THE EARTH WIRE

JOEL LANE

THE EARTH WIRE

Influx Press
London

Published by Influx Press
The Greenhouse
49 Green Lanes, London
N16 9BU
www.influxpress.com / @InfluxPress
All rights reserved.
© Joel Lane, 1994, 2020
Introduction copyright © Nina Allan, 2020

Published by Influx Press, London, 2020.
First published in the UK in 1994 by Egerton Press.

Printed and bound in the UK by TJ Books.

Paperback ISBN: 9781910312575
Ebook ISBN: 9781910312582

Proofreader: Dan Coxon
Cover design: Vince Haig
Interior design: Vince Haig

For Tim Mathias
With thanks for help in difficult times

CONTENTS

CRACKING JOKES
ON THE EDGE
OF SUICIDE:

AN INTRODUCTION
TO JOEL LANE'S *THE EARTH WIRE*

And it happens all the time. Boats go down,
cars crash, houses burn, and damaged people
spill out into the road. The only way to go
on is to realise that it is always the same.
You have to hold onto the few who mean
enough to you to bring out the healer. And
sometimes the healer is very difficult to find.
('Wave Scars', 1993)

When *The Earth Wire* was first published in 1994, I was living
and working in Exeter, where Joel Lane was born in 1963. So
associated was Joel with his adopted city of Birmingham, the
idea of him growing up in Devon was difficult to reconcile.
Exeter was my home for almost twenty years. I often wondered
where exactly Joel was born, what school he attended, where

he liked to hang out. Long before we met we had places in common. I always intended to ask Joel about his time in Exeter. I always thought there would be time. Now I'll never know.

The first story I read by Joel was 'The Lost District', which first appeared in *The Third Alternative*, a magazine of dark and strange fiction edited by Andy Cox and famous as the proving ground for many new and upcoming horror writers of our generation. It is difficult to articulate the effect his writing had on me, other than by saying I understood immediately I'd found a kindred spirit. Like so many of Joel's stories, 'The Lost District' tells of people who are damaged, who have suffered trauma, who feel deep uncertainty and ambivalence about where they might be headed. It was this sense of ambiguity most of all that drew me in, the willingness – no, the compulsion – on the part of the author to give the reader space for their own interpretation of what had happened. On the cusp of publishing my own stories, I was desperate to read more of Joel's, eager to learn more about his influences and interests as a writer.

The internet was then in its infancy, and information was sparse. The biographical note that followed 'The Lost District' informed me that Joel Lane's previous publications included a collection of short stories entitled *The Earth Wire*, but almost ten years on from when it first appeared, this obscure book from a publisher no one seemed to have heard of was long out of print, and although I scoured the shelves of every second-hand bookshop I entered I was unable to lay hands on a copy.

I went on to read Joel's newer collections as they were published, but *The Earth Wire* remained elusive, and when Influx Press announced they were reissuing the book, I realised I never had caught up with it. The invitation to write this introduction came not only as an honour, but as an almost miraculous opportunity to experience Joel's work as I had first encountered it: through stories that were new to me, as urgent and uncomfortable and ultimately transcendent as they were when they were written.

Joel Lane has come to be closely associated with a loose affiliation of mostly male British writers who rose to prominence in the 1990s. Dubbed for a time 'the miserabilists', many of them grew up under Margaret Thatcher, witnessing first-hand the rise of corporate capitalism and the consumer state, the dismantling of the nation's industrial heartland, mass unemployment and the consequent fracturing and fragmentation of working-class communities. The catastrophic material, social and cultural impoverishment that inevitably followed formed the backdrop for a new species of horror writing, a literature that steered resolutely away from the cartoonish excesses of the eighties horror boom and towards a form of weird expressionism whose influence is still felt today.

Ramsey Campbell led the way, his early Lovecraft-inflected tales soon morphing into something quite different and quite extraordinary: stories and novels in which strange and terrifying events play out amidst the quotidian post-industrial landscapes of his native Liverpool. Campbell's horror is an everyday phenomenon, freely mixing the supernatural with petty crimes of ordinary desperation. M. John Harrison, Simon Ings and Nicholas Royle (the founder of the same Egerton Press that published *The Earth Wire*) were by now also producing stories that found their centre of gravity in the stark reality of post-Thatcherism, with newer writers such as Christopher Kenworthy, Conrad Williams, Mark Morris and Mike O'Driscoll, Stephen Volk, Christopher Fowler and Graham Joyce making their own contributions to the aesthetic.

If I were to name one work that expresses the soul of this kitchen-sink weird to most seminal effect, it would have to be *The Earth Wire*. Ramsey Campbell and Mike Harrison came out of markedly different traditions (Lovecraftian horror and the New Wave of science fiction respectively), passing through miserabilism on their way to somewhere else. Many of the younger writers went their separate ways between the publication of the final issue of *The Third Alternative* in 2005 and the first issue of that magazine's successor, *Black Static*, in 2007. Joel Lane, whose literary roots lie as much in contemporary poetry as in horror fiction, continued true to the aesthetic he himself had largely created until his untimely death at the age of fifty in 2013.

What struck me most forcibly when reading the stories in *The Earth Wire* was how fully formed they are. These stories come from relatively early in Joel's career, and yet there is a maturity here, a sureness of touch, which belies that. Lane leaves the reader in no doubt whatsoever that here is a writer who knows what he wants to say, who has already begun to assemble the lexicon of themes and motifs that will come to define him. And with the distance that time brings, it is remarkable how clearly those themes reveal themselves, articulating not just this particular strand of British weird fiction but the pressing political and social issues of the day. 'Common Land' expresses the desperation and claustrophobia, the strange camaraderie that exists between victims of drug addiction. 'Thicker than Water' recalls the corrosive moral panic affecting government and the media at the time of the AIDS epidemic, as well as intuiting the first stirrings of the current wave of far-right xenophobia. 'Branded' reveals the plight of young people let down and abused by a care system on the verge of collapse, just as 'An Angry Voice' illustrates the combustible mix of anger and helplessness experienced by unemployed fathers robbed of their livelihoods and self-respect.

The backdrops to these stories – the heaps of rusting vehicles, the abandoned factories, the derelict houses, the ruined estates, the boarded-up shops – while painfully specific to time and place are equally the universal landscape of post-apocalypse. Thatcher's new urban reality is impressed on all of Lane's writing, as it is mercilessly imprinted upon his protagonists:

> Above the blackened rooftops, grey clouds stood out against the night. Jason stood next to Carol, trying to share in what she saw. Occasional lights revealed a flat wasteland where clumps of grass were mixed with various debris: rubber tyres, scrap metal, burnt plastic, coils of wire. Carol gripped his hand. Her fingers were cold, but no worse than his.
> ('Waiting for a Train', 1992)

Names occur and recur – Jason, David, Glen, Darren – as if the stories are overlapping chapters in a unified work. The period – what might now forever be called the lost district – leaps vividly to life through its minor details: the headphones on a Sony Walkman, a character reaching up to pull down the window in a train compartment, the narrative ubiquity of telephone boxes. But what marks out *The Earth Wire*, again and again, as something extraordinary is Lane's use of horror. Though there are moments and images here that are liable to shock the reader – the spectacle of 'the Wheel' in the titular story especially is not easily forgotten – the author's preferred approach is one of stealth, the kind of creeping strangeness that leaves you wondering *did that really happen?* The post-industrial Pan who leads dead men to safety in 'An Angry Voice', the fortune-teller in 'Other Than the Fair', the maimed, drowned bodies in 'Wave Scars' – Lane's feverish visions leave us in no doubt that we are down with the monsters, and that the monsters are no less deserving of pity than the rest of us.

And of all his work's attributes it is surely Joel's compassion that has been most overlooked. Whilst critics and commentators have been eager to underline the overarching bleakness of Lane's stories, they have been slower to remark upon how many of them centre upon the care of one person for another, even when they are at their most broken and mentally exhausted. Sex in Lane's stories is rarely violent, and although his characters are often too wounded and emotionally depleted to form lasting relationships, their physical intimacy is evidence of their desire not only for release but for human warmth, for connection with a fellow being, for a reason to keep on living in the world. Even when brief and unrepeated, their sexual encounters always feel meaningful. If Lane's fiction is about anything, it is about bearing witness.

———

For me personally, the stories in *The Earth Wire* offer innumerable reminders of conversations I had with Joel, emails we exchanged, also his humour, an aspect of his fiction that along with its compassion, is not often discussed. We spoke often of music – Joel's invented-band memoir *From Blue to Black* (2000) contains his finest writing, in my opinion – and in the field of folk rock especially held many albums in common. His passing mention of Dory Previn in 'Wave Scars' felt like a greeting, because who listens to Dory Previn these days, except Joel and me? 'That was the first time I'd heard that scary, desolate voice, cracking jokes on the edge of suicide,' David says, and later in the story when he travels with Steven to the Welsh coastal town of Fishguard I realise Joel must have been writing these scenes at almost exactly the same time I happened to visit the place, ten years before I published my first story, fifteen before we met. The parochial, conservative atmosphere, no cafes or restaurants that stayed open after six o'clock – these details of a provincial town in the early nineties were instantly recognisable, as were the flashes of wry, dark humour in the telling. He did not mention the cliff paths, purpled with foxgloves, but that wasn't Joel. I didn't see the phantom ship but I count that a blessing.

As I said near the beginning of this introduction, being handed *The Earth Wire* after all these years feels like something of a miracle. Now, through the perspicacity of Influx Press, I pass it on to you. As you are about to discover, Joel Lane is a unique writer, whose personal vision remains undimmed. Even though he can no longer speak to us in person, his voice remains strong.

Nina Allan, Rothesay
March 2020

COMMON LAND

She went to New Street Station to meet him. Stephen's letter had been forwarded from her old address, and he wouldn't know where to look for her. Rosalind waited outside the ticket barrier, in a brightly lit underground hall that, late at night, was filled with silent people. Some were waiting for trains, others for people walking through from the street; and others would stand until they were moved on. In his letter, Stephen had said he was homeless now. Rosalind wondered just what that meant. But the letter had a local postmark; why had he made her come here, when he could have met her in town during the day? She supposed it was one of his gestures, intended to make her feel something. Just after eleven, Rosalind thought she saw Stephen waving goodbye to someone on the far side of the ticket barrier. He came through alone, carrying a weekend bag and wearing a green overcoat that she'd not seen before, though it looked old.

He was pleased to see her. 'I didn't know if you'd be free. I've got a lot to tell you.' They walked up through the shopping arcades to the New Street ramp. Stephen was visibly tired, though he seemed inwardly worked up about something. His eyes flickered briefly at everyone who passed by. Rosalind didn't know what to ask him. Besides, she realised, the silence that had brought them face to face again might be broken by discussion. They were in time for the last bus to Northfield. The city centre seemed full of young couples, embracing in the bus shelters and shop doorways. The rain whitewashed the pavements.

Rosalind's flat – strictly speaking, a bedsit with its own sink and electric cooker – was part of one of the large houses on the main road. There was no light on the staircase. Stephen followed her up to the second floor. Inside, he stared around him as though displaced. The room was fairly chaotic; half of it was taken up by the table, on which she'd placed a large square of hardboard. This was now covered with newspaper and twisted hulks of red clay, parts of which glistened like poor special effects. Stephen sat on the couch and wrapped his arms across his chest. The stubble on his cheeks only showed up how pale his skin was. Rosalind lit the gas fire, though it was only September and she didn't feel cold herself.

'Do you remember our first year?' he said. He meant the first year at art college, when the two of them had lived in a house with three other students. They hadn't been going out together then. 'I'm trying to get another group together, like that. A commune, really. I'd like you to meet them.' He hesitated, and glanced across at the table. 'What are you doing now? Selling your work?'

'Trying to. I'm on an enterprise allowance.' They both laughed at that. Among the rough figures drying on the hardboard were a child's head with pale blue marbles for eyes and a human foot with wings growing from either side of the Achilles tendon. 'From now until next June, I'll be trying to make and sell things like these.'

'That's good. I've not done anything like that since leaving college. Actually I've been travelling around. Meeting different kinds of people.' He talked slowly, letting gaps form between his words and what he meant to say. Rosalind was just glad that he was back. Behind where he was sitting, though he hadn't noticed it, there was a painting which he'd done of her the year before last. It caught her in a rather stiff posture, closed in by an abstract grey background. She was half turned away, her features sharply defined and detailed, eyes shut. Rosalind had used to think the painting proof of Stephen's feelings for her.

'I'm not working,' he went on. 'Not officially, anyway. There's a group of us, we're moving into an empty house in Deritend, this week. It's not easy. You'll have to see for yourself, the way we live. And what the point of it is. We use whatever we can find. Like gypsies. Self-help, I suppose you could call it. That's the way I was brought up.' Stephen had come from a deprived region, one of the enclosed towns of the Black Country that had a city's landscape and a village's culture. Rosalind had a comfortable suburban background, and the differences had always stuck between them. He fell into silence. The room was warm now, the steady firelight stamping a grid on Rosalind's eyes.

'We can talk in the morning,' she said. It was ridiculous for them to have said so little to each other; but she needed to sleep, not to think. They sat on the bed under the window at the far end of the room. Stephen muttered something, thanked her for going to meet him. She unbuttoned his shirt. He was thinner than she remembered. Her hand stopped just below his ribcage, on the left side. There was something there that felt solid and cold under the skin, though the surface was unmarked. 'Does that hurt?' He shook his head. She pressed it, and thought of touching the half-frozen snow on a hedge. Her hands began to shake.

'Don't worry,' he said. 'There's nothing the matter.' He took her hands and pressed them together, then drew her head forward and kissed her, breathing into her throat. They made love very slowly and tenderly, hardly moving, as though it hurt them to draw apart. The night seemed to dissolve the building, pulling them down into each other. Rosalind felt lost; she was never at home in passion. At a rational level, she didn't believe that she had missed him this much. Stephen held her without forcing, almost childlike in his need. The thread of joy stretched tighter in the darkness, then broke, letting them slip apart from each other and into sleep.

When Rosalind awoke, her first thought was that it had somehow become winter. Stephen's breath was misted above his face, like scratches on a window. He was lying on his side, facing her; his dark hair was stuck to his forehead. His eyelids were twitching, as though his dreams were struggling towards the light. As she watched, a series of white threads drifted from his mouth and joined the cloud that was forming there. It seemed about to assume some definite shape. Stephen's mouth opened wider, and a continuous stream of fibres linked it to the slowly hardening veil that now covered his face, becoming nearly opaque.

Shocked at herself, Rosalind reached up and touched the caul. It was as soft as cotton, with harder fragments like seeds or crystals. The material did not tear, but the warmth of her hand dissolved it; soon there was nothing left. Stephen's face tensed, losing the gentleness of sleep; his eyes opened. They looked at each other. 'We need your help,' he said.

'We? You mean—'

'Me and the others.' He smiled. 'Or me and… whatever's inside. What did it look like? I mean, *who* did it look like?'

Rosalind hadn't asked herself that. 'I don't know. Not like anyone in particular. Have you seen…'

'It seems to take different shapes. From me, from other people. There are five of us. In the house.' He sat up and began to dress. Rosalind held back; she was afraid to touch him, for various reasons. Stephen made no move towards her. 'There's nothing to explain,' he said. 'What we really need is some way to form. It's no good trying on your own. We need someone who can bring it together for us. Then we'll know what's going on.' He was very nervous; Rosalind knew that he was afraid she'd reject him. She knew what he was like. Stephen broke the deadlock by putting on his coat. He took a notebook from the inside pocket, wrote something down and tore out the page. 'That's where we're going to live,' he said. 'Come and visit us, if you want to. Soon.' He kissed her goodbye; his mouth tasted quite ordinary.

Over the next fortnight, Rosalind found a craft shop in Hagley and another in Evesham that would take her clay sculptures. She began working on a series of rather delicate masks, using paler clay and a brittle varnish that made her feel lightheaded and sickly. The week after that, she went to find Stephen's house. Deritend wasn't an area where a great many people lived – or at least, not one where many people had homes. It was a district in transition between the city centre and the suburbs. Nothing old there had remained intact, but nothing had been removed either. Parts of various buildings had been taken over by wholesalers or manufacturers, who had put new signboards over the ground-floor windows while the upper storeys were left to decay, their elaborately carved roofs and windowframes stripped naked by the weather. Just off the High Street, a church had been turned into a warehouse for general works equipment; its roof now consisted of reinforced glass set in a lattice of wooden beams.

Even the A–Z map was an unreliable guide to the maze of backstreets, overlaid with railway bridges and new expressways. Series of identical terraced houses were juxtaposed with minor factories, car parks, derelict buildings, canals. Near where Stephen lived, the windows of a pub had been boarded over; someone had chalked WELCOME across one of the boards. Next to that, a scrapyard was full of cars piled three or four high and rusting steadily, like toys in the back of a cupboard. Rosalind walked under a bridge that crossed the main road, in the dip of a little valley. The sudden darkness and smell of rot made her pause and struggle to remember something. She felt displaced. The roof of the bridge was furred with black crystals. What looked like nails driven through it from above were in fact hollow pipes of lime sediment, formed by gradual seepage of water. A few of their tips glittered with an unexpected brightness, dripping.

Beyond the bridge, a line of houses faced the brick embankment of the railway. This was where the commune,

Stephen and his friends, were staying. The house was thin and crusted with the same pollution as the bridge; but the windows and their net curtains were clean. There was a small front yard where rose bushes and brambles were tangled together, obstructing the path. Rosalind knocked on the door. A middle-aged woman in a baggy green sweater opened it. 'Are you Rosalind?' she asked. Rosalind nodded, taken aback. 'Well then, come inside.' The interior of the house smelled of cooking and damp. Stephen and two younger men, who looked very like one another, were sitting in the kitchen. Stephen looked worse than he had the last time; he embraced her before speaking. Then he introduced her to the others. The woman's name was Sandra; she came from Leeds, and had been an actress. The two youths, Lee and Mike, were non-identical twins; they came from Glasgow. There was another tenant, a bearded silent man called Alan, whom Rosalind met later.

To begin with, Stephen was the only one that Rosalind had any real contact with. She came over to the house every few days, and slept with him; or sometimes he stayed over at her flat in Northfield. For Rosalind, it seemed like a chance to relive the early weeks of their relationship, now three years in the past. His illness, or whatever it was, had the effect of making him gentler and more dependent. She enjoyed taking care of him, and using the therapy to ease her own tensions and fears at the same time. He was a mirror for her, as she secretly knew and had always known. She assumed it would end, either when he recovered himself and got bored with her (as had happened before), or when she found a permanent job and moved away from the area.

If Rosalind got used to the strange material, it was only because she didn't allow anything to do with Stephen to be quite real. That was her way of not getting too involved. The sight and touch of it fascinated her. She remembered having seen photographs of seances from the nineteenth century where the same effect was produced. Stephen needed to be asleep for it to happen. She watched him in the night, until something formed out of his throat and diffused above him. It was colder than flesh, and didn't respond to air currents. Once the tissue spread across the upper half of Stephen's body, like fresh bark on a silver birch tree. It cocooned him for hours. Rosalind thought he was dying; she lay there, unable to move, until his skin was clear again.

Sometimes Rosalind thought of it as a living thing, a homeless being that had taken possession of Stephen and made him alien to her. Then she'd draw away from him, make him come to her and prove that she was needed. When they were close once more, she thought of the emissions as inert: a waste product, the traces of some unrecognisable industry. By day, she and Stephen worked together on her sculptures and pottery. They ate together, went for walks, saw films, sometimes made love. Stephen watched her all the time, obsessed as before with her image. In early December, when the frost and the shrunken daylight made travelling difficult and she couldn't afford the heating costs of her flat, Rosalind moved in with the commune.

The others accepted her, without particularly trying to make her feel at home. Rosalind and Stephen shared one room; Lee and Mike shared another; while Sandra and Alan had their own rooms. It took Sandra more than a week to start talking to Rosalind, but after that she seemed to take to the newcomer in a maternal kind of way, proving an unexpected source of advice. Her conversation was a mixture of practicality and folklore. She told Rosalind a lot about her past: travelling, the theatre, cities and lovers. Much of it was inconsistent and probably made up. But Rosalind found it strangely reassuring to think that she, too, would eventually have a past. Something else that Sandra told her stuck in her mind: that you could get a man by making a clay effigy of one and wrapping it in coils of your own hair.

One evening, when Sandra had a cold and stayed in her room, Rosalind took her up a bowl of soup. She knocked on the door and heard the answer: 'Come in.' When she opened the door, she thought Sandra was lying under a sheet. At once, her mind registered the presence of the dead. 'It's all right,' Sandra said clearly; a whitish skein lifted from her and hung between the two women, losing itself as Rosalind's eyes focused in the half-light. She felt as though her own reflection had glanced off a window or a basin of water. She knelt beside Sandra's bed, feeling giddy, and put the bowl down. The smell of boiled onions twisted in her head. The older woman reached down and took her hands, saying, 'It's all right. You're just not ready yet. Give it time.'

It wasn't until Rosalind had moved in that she realised one of the area's deficiencies. There were almost no telephone boxes. She had to walk nearly a mile towards the city centre to make a phone call. What the area did have was many public toilets, at least the small kind built into the alcoves of walls: uniform metal boxes with ornate designs on the panels. They were useless to women. By night, it was anybody's guess which buildings were derelict and which in use. Local business was a testament to the idea of self-help.

That could mean opening bed and breakfast accommodation on the ground floor of an abandoned building, leaving the upper storeys empty and blackened with half a century's dirt. Or cutting the shell of a factory down to head level, making it an enclosed scrapyard. Or using a terraced house with barred windows as a small warehouse for building materials or the like. Houses and churches were just more kinds of wall.

The dead tissue that Stephen and the others breathed limited the commune. That was how Rosalind came to see it, without being able to explain the effect. The simplicity of their lives was partly chosen and partly involuntary. They were poor, but that wasn't it. They were like patients; life had closed in on them. They worked, on and off, in the local trades. Alan was a factory's nightwatchman. Sandra cooked and served in an all-night cafe. The twins helped to load and unload trucks for the salvage department. Stephen was probably the most idle of the group; his main occupation was being the leader of their peculiar rituals. The house wasn't very fit to live in. They kept the kitchen hygienic, but the damp and grime elsewhere couldn't be dealt with. A lot of their furniture came from local rubbish tips or empty houses. They had electricity, but expense and dangerously faulty wiring deterred them from using the power points. For warmth, they depended on paraffin heaters and clothing. Rosalind tried to believe that the end would justify the means.

If only so much weren't hidden from her. One night, when she went to the bathroom to relieve herself, the washbasin was furred up with strands of ectoplasm. She tore a piece of it away; it had the feel of numbness. She could just make out her hand behind it in the dark. Another time, Rosalind tried to call Stephen's bluff. 'Why do you want me here?' she said. 'I don't belong. Nothing happens when I'm around… What does it mean? It's that different I can't talk about it or think about it. I don't know how you can live here.' Stephen faced the window, staring at the blackened wall of the embankment, the arches bricked up. 'Speak to me. Tell me something.'

He turned round and looked at her, without changing his expression. Rosalind walked out of their bedroom and down the stairs to the front door. Stephen leaned over the banister in the hallway and appeared to blow her a kiss. Clouds trailed from his hand. She spent that night in the cafe, wrapped in her depression as though it were alcohol, watching all the homeless people come, stay and eventually go. They could make a cup of coffee or a cigarette last an hour and occupy them completely. They talked in rituals, giving bits of themselves that they were used to giving, holding onto familiar phrases. *Nearly morning. Where you been? Just one more.* If you said something unexpected, they wouldn't hear you. Over Christmas, Rosalind went to stay with her father and stepmother in Stafford. They'd been living there for five years, and were gradually redecorating and refurnishing the house, so that every time she went back it was like somewhere different. She felt like a child again. What she couldn't mention seemed to get into every word she said and take away its impulse. Rather than sit in the living room and watch TV, she walked around the town, which looked unreal in its coating of frost and sodium light. For some reason, the sound of carol-singers frightened her; not the songs, but the chorus of voices. On Christmas

11

Eve they attended Midnight Mass at the cathedral. Rosalind kept thinking: *You haven't got me fooled, you two. Pretending to belong.* Her childhood hadn't been this peaceful, or this normal. It wasn't reality either.

I could tell you a few things about communion. Her last night with Stephen, she'd taken some of the plasma and tried to eat it. She'd stopped almost at once, because of the images it brought to mind. It tasted of nothing at all. She'd thought of cancer, the body eating itself. Or of primitive magic, someone eating nerves to make herself better able to feel.

Rosalind went back to the house near the end of December. In the thin daylight the countryside seemed pure and featureless, like a face that hid its age in sleep. Trees and hedges were sketched in charcoal. As the train came into Birmingham, the environment darkened. It was slightly warmer here; the veneer of frost gave way to a matt vapour. Factory chimneys bruised the clouds grey and yellow. She was thinking of Stephen. Perhaps she'd get him away from the others, soon, and the two of them could go to live somewhere in the country, say in Evesham. She wanted to hide in the privacy of their bedroom. Sculpt figures and make love with Stephen, and sleep through the long vacant nights. Everything seemed possible again.

She had to try several times before her key would turn in the lock. Evidently the cold had warped the door frame. None of the windows were lit. As she stood cursing at the front door, a goods train shuddered along the embankment behind her. Eventually Rosalind got the door open; the hall was dark. She flicked the light switch. *Fucking hell.* Either the antique wiring had given out or they'd been disconnected. Or else it was a power cut. Some light came through the windows in the kitchen. All the commune were standing in there. Just standing together, quite close, facing inward. They must have heard her struggling with the door. But even now, they ignored her. She was so angry that at first she didn't notice what they were looking at.

It was rather like the stream of ashes in the heat-haze over a bonfire. But as Rosalind watched, it took on form, becoming a kind of effigy. This time, she knew it was using her eyes to define itself. Each member of the group standing round it was connected to it at the mouth, by a glistening thread of vapour. The plasma only shone where it caught the light. Rosalind couldn't identify the figure, no matter how intently she looked at it. It had a thin body, with arms folded over its breasts, and a wreath of long hair around its face. But the face itself was somehow impersonal. The features were empty. Rosalind had the impression that they were reversed, the eyes and mouth opening inward; though that was not what she saw. It made her think of an identikit face in a newspaper; but she had never seen a female one, and found it very hard to accept this image as a woman. She pressed herself against the wall, feeling powerless, and wrapped her arms around herself in an unconscious mimicry of the creature.

The others drew back, apparently sensing that they had done what they could. For the first time, Rosalind could see how tired they were, as if they had not slept since her departure. Sandra sat down at the kitchen table and covered her face with her hands. Lee and Mike caught hold of each other and stood motionless by the window. Alan walked slowly through the doorway and up the stairs. Stephen turned towards Rosalind, reached out and touched her arm.

'Look after her,' he said. That was all he said. It was Rosalind he was speaking to. The grey-white figure settled itself on the floor, its arms around its knees; its head dropped forward. It grew fainter and lost some of its outline, but did not go away. It would not move for several hours.

More out of fear than concern for the others, Rosalind made herself do some housework. The sink was heaped with plates and cups, none of which appeared to have been used recently. She scrubbed a few clean and piled the rest on the sideboard, not knowing when they'd have some hot water. Probably the others needed a meal; she certainly did, after the journey. The only- food in the larder was dried, and months old: rice, lentils, pasta shells. There weren't even any tins. She went out to buy some fresh food and milk. When she came back, nothing had happened. She took the shirts and underclothes from the clothes-horse at the foot of the stairs, folded them and piled them up on a chair. They had dried hard, though the air had touched them with damp. She cooked some soup on the paraffin stove; its fumes nearly made her pass out.

Rosalind and Stephen ate, leaving a half-full pot on the stove for the others. The cold thing of breath and threads watched them from the floor, passively. When it grew dark outside, since they had no light, they went up to bed. Stephen fucked her twice, hard; her release was like shedding a skin. They slept huddled under the blankets. The next day they awoke after dawn; they clung together, kissing and whispering, until it was dark once more. The day after that, they got up. Rosalind washed herself and pulled clothes onto a body that still felt unreal. All the time, she knew she was being watched.

The life of the commune made more sense now. Every day, all the others would gather round the maiden-creature and breathe matter into it. The rest of the time, they hardly spoke or gave attention to anything. Rosalind felt left out. What was expected of her was something different. She talked and acted for the maiden. She couldn't talk to it, but she talked to herself or Stephen, and the thing listened. Sometimes it followed her in the house, like a voiceless double. It mimicked her posture and the movements of her hands.

Rosalind could feel everything she did or said taking on a new intensity, like performance. She relived events from her childhood, making stories of them, weaving in lines from traditional songs that she hadn't realised she still knew. The blank-faced creature took in everything. It saw her and Stephen in bed together. It saw her panic on finding a nest of silverfish in the larder, then boil water to get rid of them, and then spill the water and scald herself badly. It saw her crying, swallowing painkillers, bleeding, coughing up phlegm from a cold on her chest. This went on for nearly a fortnight.

One morning, a few days into the new year, Rosalind walked out of the house. The sunlight dazzled her; she had to keep stopping until her head cleared. The upper windows of half-ruined buildings showed her the sky. From the doorway of the cafe where Sandra worked, a man whistled at her. 'Get the message, love.' She had a toothache. A yard full of silver-headed thistles was enclosed on three sides by blocks of flats with washing hanging from the balconies. The harvest of seeds caught the light. A few hours later, when Rosalind was back in the house, she realised that she couldn't actually have seen that.

When Stephen saw she was ill, he told her: 'You'd better leave.' She ought to have known he wouldn't change. He spent more time close to the ghost-creature now, communing with it in a way she couldn't. She'd watched him kiss it, breathing substance into its blurred face. 'It's not enough,' he said. 'You have to give yourself. You can't do it. It's not your fault.' Rosalind realised that he wasn't concerned about her at all.

'What more do you want?' They were standing in the bedroom. Rosalind's face twisted with bitter emotions until it felt like a mask. Even her sense of failure was probably being used – and she didn't know for what. It was all hidden. Stephen looked out of the window, again. He was unshaven; it gave him the appearance of strength. Rosalind seized his arms and kissed him fiercely, trying to claim him. He turned away as though nauseated, and stared at the glass.

'Nothing in particular,' he muttered. 'You're not the first. And you won't be the fucking last.'

Later that day, while Stephen was out of the house, Rosalind took out a half-full bottle of vodka that she kept among her clothes in a suitcase. She drank it all, mixed with water. A strange feeling of indifference grew in her. It felt like a snow child lodged in her abdomen. She collected together whatever tablets she could find – codeine, paracetamol, a dozen or so sleeping pills prescribed a long time back. She swallowed them all, sitting on the edge of the bath, watching the water run from the tap like a stream of pure light. It took more than an hour. Finally she went back into the bedroom, drew the curtains, and lay down on the bed.

She woke up in the night, and registered only that she was alone. Before dawn, she realised that she was going to be sick. She forced herself to stand up, but didn't have enough strength to walk. She leaned her head over the bare floorboards and tried to vomit. Only a few drops of clear fluid ran from her mouth. Between that night and the next, all she could do was be sick, or try to. Twice she managed to stagger to the bathroom and swallow a few mouthfuls of water, in order to bring it up later. She was still the only one who couldn't vomit ectoplasm. In between, she lay inert on the bed and felt the hard numbness shift inside her. In spite of the cold, she was drenched in sweat.

Some of the others watched her, without trying to help. Sandra came in with Alan, and said something to him that sounded like 'No good to anyone.' The pale creature hung around most of the time. She could feel it draining her, but it pretended to nurse her. It touched her throat with its hollow fingers, and stroked her hair, making gestures of sympathy. Close up, its vacant face was a mosaic, like a cracked window; everything human in it was broken up. Rosalind vomited on its arm, a yellowish bile that scarred it deeply. Or so she thought. There was nobody to share her point of view. Stephen was nowhere in sight. He was probably out looking for someone else. Self-help was all that remained to her.

A day later, she still hadn't eaten anything. But she'd gone on drinking water until eventually she kept it down. Her face in the bathroom mirror was jaundiced. It was probably liver damage, she realised. As soon as she could keep upright, Rosalind struggled from the house and began walking towards the city centre. She could see the post office tower and clock from the roadway. It was getting dark. She watched the clouds moving overhead, a great open stretch

17

of damaged tissue. The smoke of a factory chimney reflected the light from the city. All around her, buildings enclosed the view; but she felt as though she were on a hilltop. The chill of her freedom paralysed her. What cried out in her mind, still, wasn't the atrocity half-realised in her or waiting to be fulfilled in others. It was the simple misery of knowing that the group had created something to unite them. And it had only left each of them feeling more alone.

ALBERT ROSS

Spring was overdue. It was March, and the town was still half covered with snow; that only showed how many places there were where nobody walked. The white patches were ice now, half thawed and refrozen many times over. But the air was tense with a feeling of change. That morning, Lochran had walked along the railway line near his home, following the track south-west through a countryside that was broken up by factories and mines. Before turning back, he'd waited in a tunnel while a goods train shuddered past, close enough to touch. The alcoves of the tunnel were filled in with loose bricks and dirt. The railway linked one small town to the next, but the continuity that industry had given them was dissolving. These towns and their communities were reverting to a pre-war state of isolation.

Ross called on him for the first time that evening. Lochran heard footsteps on the stairs leading down to his basement flat, and then a knock on the door. The visitor was a young man, tall and broad-shouldered, but rather thin. His nervousness seemed at odds with the need in his voice.

'You're a sort of faith healer?'

Lochran assented. He made no claims, and nobody ever came to unmask him.

'I need your help. Please. I'll explain.'

Ross introduced himself, struggling not to close off with fear. He'd come from the next town, five miles away; he worked there as a trainee electrical engineer. 'They call it apprenticeship, still. But they might as well call it a YTS, you know? Two years' work for next to nothing. And then what? I want to get away, now. My parents don't want me. But I can't do much just now about moving. You'll see why.'

As the youth moved closer to the wall light, Lochran saw that he was slightly hunchbacked. Whether that was the effect of an habitual posture, he still couldn't tell. Ross's hair was a mixture of hazel, auburn and blond streaks, as though it had been highlighted twice over. 'I'll show you,' he repeated, unbuttoning his shirt. Then, balling the shirt in one fist like a handkerchief, he stood facing the mirror on the right-hand wall of the living room. Lochran could just make out a faded tattoo across the youth's back: random lines, like crazy paving. He came closer, and saw that it represented a pattern of delicate feathers. So intricate, so detailed, that a quick glance took in only disorder.

Ross drew his shoulders forward, and the feathers tightened. 'Touch them,' he said. Lochran reached out and traced the fabric of tiny ripples and ridges under the skin. He drew his hand back; the fingertips were trembling. A tide of darkness seemed to pass through the room. 'They'll grow out in a few weeks, you know.'

Lochran stared at the thin embryo structures. They were hardly more than two-dimensional. Would they have bones? Muscles? A blood supply?

Ross shook his head; his shoulders relaxed. He put his shirt back on, and his jacket over it. Then he turned away from the mirror. 'You'll have to help me,' he said. His eyes, Lochran saw, were very dark; but their surfaces gleamed. After the youth had gone, Lochran climbed slowly up the flight of stairs to ground level. The footpath was still marked here and there with patches of frozen slush, like broken crusts thrown out for the birds. A line of poplar trees divided the avenue from the park. From a distance, they could look like giant railings. Lochran shivered and retreated to the basement flat. For the first time in years, his sleep was disturbed by the sound of the passing trains.

The next visit was nearly a month later. Ross turned up without warning, at noon on a Saturday. His grey jacket was saturated with rain, but he kept it on as he sat down and talked. 'Good day for travelling, isn't it?' he began. 'I'm leaving home tomorrow. Got some money saved up. And I'm giving up my job, too.' As he spoke, Ross combed his diversely tinted hair with his fingers, dislodging the raindrops. He looked paler and still more uneasy than before. It was odd how independence could sometimes make people regress, as though the burial of childhood had the effect of restoring it. 'Don't worry. I'll find some way to survive and make people leave me alone. I don't need my family any more. They don't know what's happening to me. Trouble is, I don't know either.'

Lochran watched the youth and waited to be told what to do. This might be his home, but it wasn't his territory any longer. Ross had brought the outside with him.

'You know why I'm here, don't you?'

Lochran nodded.

'I need your help now.'

Painfully, he stripped off his jacket and shirt. Underneath, his skin was a patchwork of dark-stained bandages. Lochran boiled a kettle and cleaned the wounds with hot water, until the cloth and bowl were a thin red. Then he began to swab the cuts with iodine. Ross quickly made him stop. The feathers were breaking out all over the youth's back.

As Lochran worked on him, Ross talked; his voice circled his own pain and anxiety, never moving beyond its orbit. 'I can't stand being in that house any more. Once I've left, I swear I'll never go back. It gets worse all the time, you know? My dad thinks he's going to lose his job. He's a spot-welder. His company's changing to a new production system that doesn't need skilled labour. And they might shut up both the local factories and move south, my dad thinks. The company's run by Americans now. They talk about new ideas and new technology. What it is, they can't stand English unions. My dad sits at home getting depressed the whole time. Reading newspapers and swearing to himself.

'My mum's just as bad in a different way. She's trying to fuss her way through it all. Never stops cleaning and cooking and worrying. She always says, if the home's taken care of then the outside world can look after itself. The more untidy my dad gets, the more she frets about keeping things in order. That and saving money. You can tell she's scared. It's like you can't breathe in the house any more. You know how cold weather turns your breath white? That's how it feels there. There's nothing I can say to them.'

While Ross talked, staring into the darkness at the far end of the living room, Lochran tied clean bandages around his back and shoulders. For the time being, all the feathers needed to be covered; the flesh around them was raw. Ross came back every few days for the same treatment. A couple of months later on, the wounds were healing over. The changes had been shockingly rapid. His back was covered with tight, colourless scar tissue; the mosaic was becoming a uniform sheet. The wings were still half covered with skin, but thin bones were pushing them up clear of the spine.

May Day had come and gone without much festivity. To the older generation it was Labour Day. But the young, even those who worked, didn't want to know about an industrial past. Their celebration, if that was the word, discharged itself through alcohol and sex. There was nothing public about it. But then, rain was the enemy of openness. It made you keep indoors; or if you faced nature, you did so covered up and facing downward, protecting your surface. Lochran thought repeatedly about escape. Images, not plans. He watched birds criss-crossing the railway like stitches; in his mind, he watched Ross flapping down the length of the sunken canal in the evening. Lochran had always depended on other people to do his dreaming for him.

And about twice a week, Ross was there, needing to be cleaned and bandaged. And listened to. There was a lot of actor in him. Lochran knew from experience that listening was the most reliable part of healing, if not the easiest. Ross seemed to be regenerating himself, becoming sharp and raw. Perhaps he was losing his father's shadow. Sometimes he talked about flying, in the mountains further north. He'd been up there before: the air was thin and clear, making

23

tissue of breath. Ross thought he could glide, at least. When he was stronger, perhaps he'd bring Lochran with him through the air.

In early summer, Ross seemed to be weakening. His voice was uneven, and once he stumbled on the steps outside Lochran's door, nearly falling. A flight of stairs is the only flight you'll ever make, Lochran thought. Then Ross showed him how to help. By then, he could raise the wings near the level of his head, exposing the hollows of incomplete flesh at their base. Lochran put his fingers to the dark spots, under the half-extended wings; the fingertips sank in. At once he felt a dull pain in his hands, and his vision began to blur and brighten at the same time. The wings were flickering like a candle flame. Perhaps the neon tube in the wall was defective. When Ross pulled away, Lochran saw the whorls of tiny cuts in his fingertips, close to the nails. They were closing already.

That night, Lochran dreamed he was standing with Ross on a hillside. The wings spread over their heads, sharing matter with the clouds. They beat slowly and powerfully, lifting him clear from the ground. The two men spiralled together above a town which Lochran recognised as his present home, though its setting was entirely different. Ross brought him downward slowly, shifting from one air current to the next. As they neared the ground, the layers of movement converged. Lochran awoke struggling for breath.

All the next day, the air seemed too scarce for activity. All he could do was wait for Ross to come back. The strip light in the living room was flickering, like a strobe. It made the room as unfamiliar and impersonal as a nightclub. When Ross didn't turn up in the evening, Lochran felt helpless. He went for a walk alongside the railway line. It was still daylight; but feathers kept blurring his view, like specks of dust on a lens. He stood on the bridge over the tunnel, waiting until he felt the train shake the world. So this was the inconceivable change. That his home town should have become that 'somewhere else' where his life could open up and be passed through by another.

Ross must have planned it like that, from the outset. The new factor in the treatment seemed to help the growth of the wings. Ross wore a large knapsack on his back now, cut open to store them. Lochran realised that the wings were vestigial; though perhaps they were not yet fully grown. The drawing of blood became a ritual, as the wings grew stronger and better defined. The feathers dried, hardened, took on colour: a chestnut brown with flecks of silver and black, like leaves mixed with ashes.

Summer passed without an excess of sunlight or warmth.

Lochran didn't treat many patients these days. He went back to pottery and sculpture, to make some money. When he realised how marked and shaky his hands were, he became frightened. He told Ross the treatments had to end. The youth nodded. 'I understand. Don't worry.' Lochran didn't see him for a fortnight. Then he turned up near midnight, his face dull with shock. He had to hold onto the door frame to keep upright. 'They saw me,' he said. 'A bunch of lads, biking it through the forest. I was asleep, somewhere I thought was out of sight. They woke me up, and then – I couldn't run. The wings got in the way. They pulled me down and started hitting me, kneeing me in the back. But quiet like, not really hard. When I stopped moving they just went away. Maybe they were afraid of killing me, it would have made me real.'

The damage wasn't as bad as Lochran feared. Some little bones were smashed, and the feathers were torn. Lochran kept him in the basement flat for a week, after Ross admitted that he usually slept out of doors now. It was easy to feed and nurse him, treating the wings simply as a peculiar sort of wound. Did they feel strange to him? Lochran asked once. It wasn't meant as a simple question, and Ross paused before answering. 'No. Whatever happens, it's still me. But they make the world different. True?'

Lochran tried to restore the wings with the blood of pigeons. He went out at night through the park and along the railway, with an air-rifle and an electric torch, looking for sleeping targets. It was an awkward and dangerous activity. And it didn't work. Eventually, Lochran decided to give up his own blood. His hands shook with fear as he placed them under the youth's wings. The pain was dulled by a sense of unreality. Obscure visions pressed behind his eyes, like a magic lantern show. They must be things Ross had seen or imagined. Dark rooms. Parents standing in a doorway. A fabric of trees. The torture of muscles, blood vessels, skin, all taking on a shape not figured in the mind. Bones turning soft, then hard and sharp. Falling, hitting the ground, getting up, running.

Abruptly, the wings spread out: wide ripples of auburn tissue, nearly filling the room. Lochran slumped forward against Ross and kissed the back of his neck, the tiny hollow at the base of the skull. Ross arched his back and brought his face against Lochran's mouth. They stayed like that, kneeling, for another hour. In the flickering light, the shadows made the room seem full of people. At the far end of the room, Lochran's handmade bowls and vases and incomplete clay sculptures were grouped on a long table: a dimly perceived and lifeless community, beyond reach.

As he recovered, Ross became able to rest; and his exhaustion, for so long caged in by habits of tension, began to work through his system. He spent the days huddled by the fire, his face dark with inner questions. He slept on the couch, though he and Lochran might have shared a bed if Ross's wings hadn't needed, in their damaged state, to be undisturbed. One morning, Lochran awoke to find himself alone in the flat. Ross had left no message, except for placing a book from Lochran's shelves, an anthology of poems, on the table. There was a bookmark at a poem of William Empson's. Lochran blinked at the words, trying to gather the scarce light of early dawn. Empson was hardly the most readable of poets. Then he saw that Ross had put a faint cross, in pencil, by the lines: *Till you have seen what a threat holds below, / The heart of standing is you cannot fly.* From that point, Lochran began to rebuild his life.

Starting with his hands, which had to be not only healed but re-educated, taught how to work. Lochran destroyed many bowls and figures before his fingers would co-ordinate with his eyes. Perhaps his eyes were part of the trouble. Their standards had changed. With the transition from British Summer Time to the real autumn, Lochran started to cut himself off from his surroundings. He found a job making pottery for a shop in the Midlands – the first regular craft job he'd had in ten years. If he moved down there, he could combine the job with working in the shop itself. He made the relevant arrangements, but left his preparations for travelling as late as possible.

On the fifth of November, Lochran went to see the firework display in the park. There wasn't much to it. The fireworks were noisier but less eye-catching than those he remembered from childhood. Afterwards, most of the crowd dispersed; but the bonfire was still encircled by people. Most of them were local youths; they were staring into the fire as if they could store its heat within themselves. He saw the same youths by day, sitting around the shopping centre or the public library. Factory closures were choking the town.

The same week, Ross came back. He was thinner and more fragile, hardly more than a child. Without speaking, he slumped at the table. His face was broken with unhappiness. Lochran cooked him some food. Once Ross started talking, it all came out in a rush. 'I'm back at home now… Need to save up enough money to get my own place. It's worse than ever at home. There's no going near my dad now. He just ignores you. If you make him notice you then he makes you regret it. And my mum's getting frantic. She spends half her life on the phone. Talking to her friends, anyone who'll listen. Phones the Samaritans and goes on half the night. I don't know who's going to crack up first, my mum or my dad. When the phone bill arrives there'll be hell to pay, I tell you. The roof'll come off that house.'

Ross was working again, on a night shift. He was a porter at the big hospital due east of the town. 'I'd sooner it was a normal hospital. It's full of mental patients. Some of them make trouble at night. Trying to get out, or start a fight, or kill themselves. I know how they feel, sometimes. But sitting in there of a night, you don't *want* to know how they feel. You want to keep your mind outside. You know?' He might get moved to an early morning shift soon. He didn't want to apply for a disability allowance, though he could get one. At work, he passed as a hunchback.

'Look what it's like now.' Ross took his shirt off and crumpled it fiercely. The wings had dried and begun to shrink. They didn't look capable of moving. Quickly, he pulled his shirt back on. Lochran told him about the new job and moving south. 'Can I come with you?' the boy asked.

'What for?' Lochran said, staring at the dull pieces of clay on the table.

'To be with you. I don't want your hands. Or your blood, not any more. I just want you. Is it too much to ask?'

Another healing, Lochran thought. *Yes, too much.* He shrugged.

'It couldn't work out. What we both need is a new start. Not to try and hold onto the past.'

Ross was silent for a while. Then he smiled. 'Come off it. You need me. Don't you? I can't see you leaving me.' Lochran turned away, facing the dusty mirror on the near wall. His chest tightened with anger and fear. He saw his own pale face, thinning hair, damaged hands. The fingerprints were scarred over. He saw indistinctly: his eyesight had grown weaker. Even as his vision had grown more demanding. He saw how he had aged while Ross had grown younger. The wings had distracted his attention from that other, no less strange process. Lochran's destination was age, but Ross was heading back towards childhood.

'You know,' he said at last, that was true until you said it.'

Ross sat on the couch, defeated. His shoulders hunched, reminding Lochran of the wings. Then his eyes closed, and his face became peaceful. Lochran gripped the boy's shoulder and shook him gently. It was past midnight. 'Sleep on the bed. I'll be up a while yet.' Ross lay on his side, knees drawn up, arms crossed over his chest. Lochran walked around the room, looking for something to do. He felt like an accessory. There was no organising principle within him.

He tried to make a list of his possessions, and to plan their packing and transport. Then he looked at Ross, leaned over the bed and whispered: *It's over. It's over.* He stood there, looking past the sleeping figure at the window. He'd forgotten to draw the curtains, and the night was a blur across the glass; the light in the room, poor as it was, prevented him from seeing anything outside.

THE CLEARING

It was still dark when Martin awoke, but by the time he was dressed, there was as much daylight as a day like this would have. As the nights became longer, the transitions became more rapid. Usually, on a Saturday morning, he would have caught up with the world at his own pace, with the help of the newspaper and the radio. But today there was no paper yet. The milk was late, too; and he had none left in the fridge. Breakfast would have to wait. Besides, there was a question in his mind that called for an answer. He had dreamed something about Phil; what, he couldn't remember, but if he kept moving it might jump back into his mind. His friend wanted to tell him something. Martin would have to go and visit him; he knew Phil wasn't on the phone any more. What made him put on his coat and go wasn't the expectation of recovering whatever Phil had been going to say in his dream. It was the thought that the only way to know whether Phil were still alive was to go straight to his house. Nobody outside could know.

The streets were deserted. Martin had never really noticed before how much nature was visible in this part of the city. It was because nature was changing: autumn discriminated among the trees, making some flare up and burn out while others remained a slick green. But the city was changing too. This district was losing its population; old property was being evacuated and demolished, to make way for hotels and office blocks. Soon it would be a place where many worked and stayed, but nobody had a home. For now, the rows of little council-built houses were shut up, looking fragile against the white sky. A flock of black wedges passed overhead in unstable formation.

Martin waited alone in the bus shelter. He felt a longing for substance that was most easily interpreted as hunger. But nowhere seemed to be open; there were lights in the windows above the corner shop, but the blinds were drawn below. A thin pale object was hanging from the lamppost outside the shop. Martin realised, with a shock, that it was a dog. Blue twine was awkwardly knotted round its neck. It smelt of cold but nothing else. Martin's curiosity struggled with his horror of touching the animal. He wasn't used to looking at dead things, and so it took him a while to realise that it had been beaten to death. Its spine and skull were crushed, and its limbs hung down in the odd postures imposed by shattered bones. One of the gangs of youths that roamed the estate by night must be responsible. One of the dog's forelimbs was unnaturally short, he noticed. Perhaps that deformity had prompted them to kill it. He walked back to the bus shelter and waited; a few cars hurried past. He'd have to walk, then; if something was the matter, at least he could find out what in the town centre.

On the way, he saw another flat being cleared out. It was on the ground floor of a three-storey building. Two young men in greyish uniforms were carrying furniture from the door to the back of a van. Something in their clothes, buttons or badges, caught the light and glittered. Martin hurried on before they could notice him watching. When he crossed the bridge over the canal, it felt as though he were escaping an island. The little housing estate, built decades ago in the era of public services, no longer had any force within itself to make for survival. It was isolated from the city not only by water, but by time and a kind of quarantine. Nobody would move in there to settle down. The cancer problem seemed worse there, too. Of course, the papers talked about the 'poverty drift' that concentrated the poor and unhealthy in certain areas. But perhaps there was some kind of local pollution. It felt like that. Too many homes were being evacuated and sold off, the sick forced into the massive public hospitals where they couldn't last long.

You couldn't tell, these days, who might be dying. People mostly kept to themselves, locked in with television and a shelf of videos that kept the past alive. A few solitary individuals still wandered around on foot, too far gone in age or alcohol to be aware of the changes. Then there were the gangs; nothing organised, just clusters of youths on the prowl for anything they could possess or hurt. This early in the morning they'd be asleep. On the bridge, Martin turned and gazed back over the mosaic of roofs. He couldn't dislodge his feeling that something new had taken the housing estate by night.

But the town centre was much the same as ever: a busy confusion of lights and sounds. Even here, Martin realised, most of the activity was artificial. Multiple faces worked on television screens in shop windows; video displays advertised today's bargains. Music pulsed from the doorways of fashion shops, where dummies wore intensely coloured fabrics. He stared at a pale blue shirt, whose pearl buttons reflected the glare of an overhead light. For a moment he had a sensation of real hunger: to touch, to be held. Further up the road, a newspaper vendor sat in a tiny shed, half asleep. She blinked at him in doubt when he held out the money for a paper.

As usual, there was nothing in the news about the deaths, or the changes that pressed behind them. The closest item was something about new projects for the redevelopment of run-down areas; instead of describing what was happening to the tenants, the article talked about restoring social organisation. The word 'discipline' caught Martin's eye; but he couldn't be bothered to read on. There was some news about violence in Europe, and a lot of advertisements. Folding the newspaper away in his coat pocket, Martin saw a bus pass by nearly empty. Well, at least some were running. But if he were going to call on Phil, he might as well walk the rest of the way and save the fare.

The theme of housing continued to play on his mind as he passed from the town centre to another suburb, less derelict than his own but still notably subdued. He walked by several building sites, where unfinished facades held up frames of scaffolding half clothed in shiny tarpaulins. The death rate wasn't quite keeping pace with the demolition. Healthy tenants couldn't be evicted if they paid the rent;

so property owners put up their rents until they had forced everyone out. Of course, sick tenants were being evicted all the time. A couple of years ago, the hospitalisation of cancer victims had been made compulsory. That had been the turning point, Martin supposed: when a popular fear had been made into law. And that was roughly when the massive project of urban redevelopment had got under way. *The clearing*, Martin thought; the phrase seemed to be related to his dream about Phil. He doubted that these new buildings would be any safer or more habitable than the old. That was if they were even meant to be lived in. Perhaps, like the hospitals, they were meant for the dying.

It was nearly midday when he reached Phil's house. No lights were on indoors. He rang the bell; there was no response. Perhaps they'd been evicted. The thought made him ring again, furious at his lack of knowledge. This time an unfamiliar face appeared briefly at the window. Then the door opened, and Sally was standing there. 'Come in,' she said quietly. He waited in the hall while she locked and bolted the door after him.

Phil's wife looked so tired and pale that Martin could understand why he'd failed to recognise her face in the window. She looked at him and nodded. 'Phil died three days ago.' In the living room, Ruth was sitting immobile on a couch in front of the television. She must be eight years old now. Her eyes did not shift as Martin crossed the doorway.

'I'm sorry,' he said. 'I wish I could have known.' But Phil's death meant another question. 'What happened? Is he buried?' It seemed an indecent question to ask; but Sally didn't seem to be offended by it.

'We'll talk about it later,' she said. Martin followed her into the kitchen. The smell of cooking made him dizzy; a black grid pressed against his sight. He leaned against the wall and shut his eyes. 'Are you all right?' she asked, concerned. 'You've gone very pale.' When he opened his eyes, the dark streaks slowly dissolved.

'Just tired,' he said. 'I walked here. And I haven't eaten today.' Some kind of vegetable soup was boiling on the stove.

'You're welcome to stay for lunch,' she said, turning back to her preparations. Keeping busy must be helping her to stay in control. She had withdrawn into the task of keeping herself and Ruth alive. Martin reflected that he was no longer Phil's friend to her so much as a part of the outside world; offering him food was a way of making him safe. It came as a shock to him to realise how badly he needed that domestic comfort himself. Sally cut three pieces from a loaf and called Ruth in. The three of them ate in silence at the kitchen table.

Mother and daughter had the same withdrawn look, a false calm he'd seen before in the bereaved. Anything he said might be a cue to release their terror. Even his presence here was a threat; the two looked only at each other. Martin had always been by himself, relatively speaking. He'd never experienced a loss that had reduced him in this way. Indeed, during the worst phases of his life he did not really seem to have been there. That was what getting over something meant, after all: to put something outside yourself, to make it less real. Perversely, he envied Sally her grief, or rather the reality that it belonged to. Nobody would come to him needing to be fed.

When they had finished, Sally sent the child up to her room. Then she sat facing Martin, preparing herself to talk. 'Phil was killed,' she said at last. 'He wouldn't have died for weeks yet, even months. He was still talking to me, even though he could only whisper. You know, I used to think cancer was when the mind turned against the body. But Phil was so involved with life. Whatever was destroying his body had nothing to do with him.' There was a pause. Martin knew what she meant. He and Phil had been close friends for five years before Phil's marriage and nine years since; they had studied together in college. There was more of Phil's thought in Martin's than he could begin to unravel. The memory of what he'd dreamed the night before slipped back into his mind. Before he could hold onto it, Sally spoke again.

'I was at work, of course. I had to leave Phil with only Ruth to look after him. It was risky enough, her missing school. You know we had to keep anyone from finding out. You were one of the few people outside who knew. But if he'd been taken into the hospital, that would have been the end. You know, people say that they're actually killing everyone who goes in there. Since they're all going to die anyway. It's a waste of resources to take care of them.' Sally was speaking in a rapid undertone; he couldn't even nod in reply. He'd not heard her talk like this before: so clear and yet defeated, as if her thoughts belonged to some impersonal public horror. 'Do you remember when people used not to behave as though the cancer was contagious? In those days, they used to talk about what caused it. Was it the bombs in the East, or pollution, or biological warfare, you know. It was really the terror that was catching. Now, people only seem concerned with getting rid of the victims. They won't even let you bury your dead. I was going to bury Phil in the garden, you know, at night. I think the silence made it harder for him to go on living. He wasn't one to keep quiet.'

Sally relapsed into silence, bitterly. She glanced up the stairs, as if to confirm that Ruth was out of earshot. Then she caught Martin's eye. No, he thought. Not if it's that bad. Tell me he died of cancer. He didn't want to be the only living adult she trusted.

'I came home from work on Wednesday. The door was wide open. Ruth was sitting on the stairs alone. I couldn't get her to move or speak. She still won't say anything about what happened. They'd gone through the house, stolen a few things. What they could carry away easily, I suppose. And they'd killed Phil. One of his hands was in the hallway. Ruth was staring at it. They'd left some part of his body in each room of the house. It was an efficient job. There was no unnecessary mess. It must have taken a few people to do it. They'd put his head up in the attic, so I'd find it last of all.'

Martin began to tremble helplessly. He pressed his fingernails into his scalp and let the shuddering pass from the back of his neck to the muscles of his face. There were no tears. Whenever he looked at Sally, the terror caught hold of him again. At last his head fell forward onto his arm. He wanted to sleep. He stood up, turned away, reached for his coat and couldn't turn back. 'Look, thanks for coming round,' Sally said. If she could find the strength to say that, then he could turn round. He faced her.

'Is there anything I can do?'

She shook her head. 'Not really. I'll go back to work on Monday. I've been here the last two days. The house is clean now.'

'Maybe you should leave for a while.' Even for good, he thought. He realised he wanted to escape from the city.

'No,' she said. 'Can't leave my job. And Ruth has her school.'

'I'm leaving home,' Martin said on impulse. 'Going north. Maybe to Scotland.'

Sally shrugged. 'Good luck, then.'

'Take care.' After she had let him out, he could hear her bolting the door.

On the way back, Martin pieced together his dream as if it had been his last contact with Phil. Somehow it had been in a forest. Was that what had put Scotland into his mind? He and Phil were students again, on holiday somewhere. They were walking through a thick forest at nightfall. He could only just make out Phil's tall figure a few feet ahead of him. As the path narrowed, darkness filled in what spaces remained between and above the trees. Eventually they had stopped. The patches of dim light were so vague and fragmented that they looked like optical illusions. When can we stop? Martin asked. Where is the clearing? There had to be somewhere where they could see each other, instead of walking in single file. Where they could lie down on even ground, look up and see the sky. Phil didn't answer. Passing back through the static city in the afternoon, Martin answered the question for himself. The clearing is wherever you can stand up. That was what his friend would have said. Perhaps he could have told his dream to Sally. Wherever you can stand up and not be alone.

There was no more human activity in the city than before. Martin was near the bridge over the canal when his way was blocked by a large group of youths. They were all dressed in the same silvery-grey uniform as the two men he had seen that morning. They seemed in a hurry, but vaguely organised; they were almost marching. One was carrying a radio. It was as though they were trying to be soldiers, but didn't know how. When they reached him, he stepped aside; not far enough to please one of them, who caught him on the arm with a heavy elbow. When another seemed to have the same intention, Martin took shelter in a shop doorway. Where had everyone else got to? As the stiff figures passed by, he noticed that their uniform was of some grey fabric with tiny silver grains, like highlights. Soon the group was diminished in the perspective of the white sky and the vertical buildings fringed with scaffolding.

On the other side of the bridge, in order to avoid the lamp post with the hanging dog, Martin took a shortcut past the church. The graveyard, he could see through metal railings, was long disused and overgrown. But had it been so badly vandalised before? Scarcely a headstone remained standing. The odd random assault on such monuments was familiar enough. But this looked like a systematic attempt at destruction. The sight made him feel unsafe. He thought of Sally's remark: They won't even let you bury your dead. The privacy of Phil's death had been taken from him. Shut them up and cut them up, he thought with a note of hysteria. It was getting dark already. An unfinished moon was just visible in the clouds above the rooftops.

The lights in Martin's house were on; the door was open. When he walked inside, he could hear footsteps upstairs. He went to the top of the stairs. A young man in grey clothes was going from room to room, looking into each one. He glanced back, saw Martin, and carried on. 'It's all right,' Martin said. 'Nobody's dying here yet.' As he was going down the stairs, another youth crossed from the living room into the kitchen. He was carrying Martin's radio and a carrier bag. The silver flecks in his uniform caught the dying light from the front doorway. Martin stood in the kitchen and watched him clearing the food from the cabinet, the shelves, the fridge. It didn't take long. Rage swirled in Martin's head like a mist of sparks. He envied the intruder's youth and his sense of knowing what to do. At last he spoke: 'Why are you taking things?'

The answer came: 'Scarcity of resources.' As the youth stepped past him, Martin saw that his hair, which was cropped close to his skull, was bleached. He felt taunted by his own passivity. The other came down the stairs, carrying a small clock. The two left immediately, leaving the front door open behind them. Martin caught sight of his own pale face in the hall mirror and slammed his fists hard against his cheekbones. The pain calmed him down a little.

He walked around the house, checking what had been moved or taken. There was nothing here for him to eat. Had they assumed that he was going to die; did they know something that he didn't about disease? Was this what a house looked like when it had cancer in it? Martin paced from room to room, examining every pale surface with suspicion: walls, sheets, mirrors, clothes, newspapers. There was a cold vacant feeling in his mind. He was afraid to touch anything, or even to stand still here. He could see inertia holding him in the house, forcing him to close the curtains, pinning him down in his bed. He packed a few things in a rucksack, put on his overcoat and went out, leaving the house open to the night.

Near the bridge, figures were busy on the canal towpath. Two men in grey came down from the back of a van, wheeling a trolley between them. Two others were tipping the contents of a similar trolley into the water. Martin stood on the bridge, looking down onto the length of the canal. For as far as he could see, the still water surface was made uneven by floating objects. The odour of petrol hung above the dark, half-submerged forms, which were wrapped in something like sacking. He looked back towards the housing estate: there was no sign of activity in the streets. It was as though the place he was leaving had been written off.

The streets on the other side of the bridge were brightly lit and crowded with people. From this distance he could not see where they were all going. A flicker of light from the canal made him look back down. They had been set on fire. Flames ran jaggedly over the darkness between the stone banks. Most of the bodies did not catch fire properly; heat exposed them, made them shift, but could not settle inside them. Ribbons of black smoke escaped from them, as from fireworks. There was a beautiful confusion of colours where petrol mixed with water. Martin felt suffocated with anger and disgust. Let them all burn. The heat stung his legs as he crossed to the opposite bank.

Close up, he still couldn't see where everyone was going. Some were in pairs or little groups; most were alone. None of the youths in silver-grey were in evidence. Martin ran from one street to another, looking for someone who might know what was going on. He was the only one running. Nobody was carrying anything, or doing anything other than walking. He stopped a man at random and asked him what was happening. The man mumbled something and turned away. He stopped another, asked again. 'Under,' was the response. 'Going under' – and the speaker was gone.

It took Martin a few minutes to recognise what the answer referred to. Here and there, in a random way, the pedestrians were taking shelter. Some were going down into subways and staying there. Others crowded into bus stations, empty buildings, even narrow alleys. A small patch of waste ground where a house had been demolished was filling up with silent people. What were they looking for: food, lost possessions, other people? The silence suggested a total lack of intention.

Away from the main street the lamp posts were less frequent. The moon was blurred behind clouds. Martin drifted with the others down the middle of the road, flanked by two lines of parked cars. It reminded him of the canal. No traffic seemed to be moving. He felt the vacancy within himself growing in oblique sympathy with his companions. He was one of the public, after all; he was not a carrier of disease. They did not need to be quarantined. They had nothing inside them to die of, or to die with. Disease was the city. All around him now, lamplight and moonlight stretched pale skin over walls and pavements. The pedestrians were little patches of darkness, searching for hiding places.

Scar city of resources, Martin whispered. Skin, the scripts for a silence. Bones, the keys to the isolation room. Blood, discharged without honour. Tissue, we all fall down. The sound of regular footsteps was all he could hear. He passed in the stream of figures down a flight of stone steps, into an underground car park. Many people were already standing there. A faulty neon light jittered overhead, giving the illusion of change. Martin walked on until he found a place that was nearly dark and quite still. Others gathered round him; somebody touched his hand, then drew away. He let himself become surrounded.

After an hour or so, a new sound became audible: a low murmur that filled the well of half-light. Martin felt his own throat moving in accord. With a vague insight that slowly brightened into recovered knowledge, he realised what they had come here for. They were looking for the deaths that had been taken from them. When the dead were massed or dismembered, people could no longer touch death within themselves. There was no register for the body's time. What this gathering voiced was only a wordless protest against silence, a shared regret that mourning was impossible. Nobody lit any matches. But at least they were together, down here, and not in single file.

THE NIGHT WON'T GO

The first real day of winter was the day he put on the wrong clothes. He'd stood for ten minutes in the shower, trying to wash away his hangover. Going back into the dark bedroom, he'd reached into the chest of drawers on the left-hand side of the bed. Daniel's clothes were hardly distinguishable from his own; they often swapped T-shirts or sweaters when one of them ran out. Without putting the light on, Peter dressed himself in Daniel's shirt and trousers. The fabric was briefly as cold as glass. The mirror showed him only a blurred figure, like a shadow.

He didn't know what he was doing it for. But it couldn't do any harm. It wasn't as though the other were dead, or even seriously ill. Most of Daniel's clothes were at the hospital now. These were probably what he'd wear if he came back to stay for a few days. When he came back. Peter left the flat, unable to face breakfast; he took some coffee in tablet form. Outside, the pavements were smeared with frost, like the residue of a million cars' exhaust fumes. On the bus, he watched people folding themselves inward, keeping their faces tight against the cold. If you wanted to, you could get through winter without really living through it. Just by dressing warmly, or staying in warm places. You could get through anything in that way.

Two or three times a week, he visited Daniel at the hospital. It was in Longbridge, an unreal building of concrete and reinforced glass. The interior walls were painted a faint blue, and the strip lighting seemed not to cast any shadows. Sometimes Daniel was sitting in the TV room; sometimes he lay on his bed, staring at the wall. It wasn't that he was really gone, not all the way through like some of them. And he wasn't drugged except to help him sleep. He just needed to be alone most of the time. Peter never knew what to say to him. It was no good pretending with Daniel, who could remember everything that had happened perfectly well. Sometimes Peter wondered if he was the main reason why Daniel didn't just stand up and go home.

A week into December, they talked about it. The other day room, next to the TV room, had a coffee machine and a line of pot plants under the windows. You were allowed to smoke in here. People dropped cigarette-ends in the flowerpots, though there were heavy steel ashtrays on the tables. The windowpane was shielded by a layer of polythene that creased the light. Peter said he'd be spending Christmas at his parents' in Lincoln. 'You could come with me,' he said to Daniel, who stared at him as though he'd suggested a trip to the moon. 'They won't mind. They like you.'

Daniel jerked forward in a way that made Peter flinch involuntarily; then he laughed. 'Peter, how old am I?'

'Same age as me. Twenty-two. You know that.'

'But *you* don't. If I wasn't in here, you wouldn't be speaking to me now. How would you take me to your parents'? In a suitcase? Red Star delivery?'

'I don't understand.' Peter felt something catch his breath, like a chill in his lungs. He started to cough.

'You're bad enough on your own. With your family round you, you won't be human.' Suddenly, Daniel smiled at him. 'Nobody is.' He grasped Peter's hand, and they sat like that for a while, letting the silence pull them together. Daniel had always gone in for what a friend of Peter's called knight's-move thinking: two steps forward, one step sideways. It wasn't new; but Peter seemed to have become less tolerant of it. Now he had a reason for not trying to understand it. Perhaps more than one reason. Before Peter left, they agreed that Daniel would come back to the flat for the New Year, if not before. On the way home, Peter felt his senses briefly open to the world. He tasted a mixture of woodsmoke and carbon monoxide in the frosty air. Across the road, a brazier was burning in a corrugated-iron shelter, drawing the night in close to its red-gold shapeless wound. It was a strange and uneasy moment, more like childhood than anything Peter had been through in the last ten years.

The fortnight before Christmas was a difficult time at work. For once, the distraction from schedules and production quality was shared by the management. The sense of things left undone created a brittle atmosphere. Peter sat at his desk by the window in the overheated office, trying to look busy. Each day seemed to fall like the snowstorm in a paperweight.

He was working through the last stages of preparing a thick study text in market research. Each chapter had to be proofread, passed through to the typesetters, rechecked, illustrated with diagrams, and then collated. The office was on the third floor of a late-Victorian block with a cramped spiral staircase and no lifts. In the windows of the buildings opposite, he could see clouds reflected: dark-grey masses, edged with silver in the weak sunlight.

Each day was shorter than the one before. The dark seemed to have a momentum of its own that pressed behind everything. Whenever Peter went out, the pubs were filled with people he hadn't seen in months or years. At home, he felt displaced by the cold and the flat's general deterioration. He couldn't afford to keep the heating on, even when he developed quite a bad cold. Aspirin kept his symptoms under control, and after a few days of it he wasn't sure what was infection and what was just the effect of being depressed. His head felt like a closed furnace. Partial voices broke inside it at night, like fire crawling under white ashes. A few times, when he was drunk, Peter took Daniel's guitar out of its case in the bedroom and plugged it in. The echoing chords seemed to reassure him, though he couldn't play nearly as well as Daniel.

Walking around Moseley at night could take away any sense of reality. Many of the houses were a century old, not beautiful but strongly designed, and warm with shadows. Some had rusty fire escapes attached to the side walls. Front-room windows displayed bookcases, heavy furniture, paper lampshades lit up like full moons; above the wide arches of plate glass, the crests of the windows were mosaics of deep colour. The trees in front gardens were like sculptures, energy frozen in their still bodies.

On the High Street, shops were awkwardly made up with tinsel, glitter-paint and paper streamers. The red effigy of Santa Claus in a clothes shop window contrasted strangely with slim, elegant dummies. In a craft shop, Peter saw a bone-white enamel mask that he thought would make a good present for Daniel. A few years ago, shopping for gifts had seemed exciting. Now he could see how things were being sold. His job was partly to blame for that. Whenever he walked through the city centre during the day, he was reminded of a quote from some market research journal: 'In the factory we make cosmetics, in the drugstore we sell hope.' Just now, the city centre was impenetrable with crowds. The same anonymous songs played everywhere, creating the effect of a whispering gallery.

One Sunday afternoon, there was a sharp knock at the door of Peter's flat. He knew it was someone who hadn't visited before; otherwise, whoever it was would have rung the bell from downstairs. But when he opened the door, he thought for a frightening moment that Daniel was standing there. Of course, it was Ian, Daniel's brother. There were only a couple of years between them. 'Come in.' Peter felt shamed by the disorder of the flat. Ian stood in the doorway, the left arm of his coat hanging empty. Underneath, he was still wearing a plaster cast and a sling. Like Daniel, he was tall and sharply featured. Peter looked at him in an uneasy way that was part displaced affection, part fear. Ian smiled to himself.

'Where's Daniel?'

'Still at the hospital,' Peter said. 'He'll be out soon.'

'Right. Well, perhaps it's good that he's not here. We're hoping he'll leave us alone over Christmas.'

Peter felt his sympathy towards Ian dissolve. 'I'm sure

49

he wouldn't want to disturb you. He's sorry about what happened. So am I.'

Ian shrugged. 'It's been coming for years. Daniel never had much self-control. Nobody wants a feud. Just tell him to stay away.'

'Yeah, I will. How's your arm now?'

'Healing. Can't do my job, though.' Ian was a National Express coach driver. 'Listen, I've come to give you some things. They belong to Daniel.' He raised a plastic bag, half filled with papers. 'Things he left with Mum and Dad, in his old room. They're clearing it out now. A few books, letters, photographs. He's probably forgotten about them.'

Peter took the bag. It was fairly light. 'Thanks.' He was sure Ian's trip hadn't been necessary. Daniel had told him what Ian was like. But Peter didn't want another argument. Nor did he want any kind of reconciliation with this near-stranger who looked like Daniel. 'Have a good Christmas,' he added, trying not to sound ironic.

'And you. Look after him.' Ian stared into the narrow emptiness of the flat. 'Everybody needs someone, don't they? Or they think they do. Even if it's only someone to hurt.' He stepped back and hesitated, then reached for the door handle with his right arm. Peter suddenly realised that Ian was left-handed. 'Take care.' The door closed. Peter walked around the flat as the dark began to press in through the windows. He played a Kitchens of Distinction album loud enough to shout down Ian's voice in his head. He cleared the table and sideboard, washed up, vacuumed the floor, took out the rubbish. He tried not to think.

It didn't snow that winter, but there were a few chilling

rainstorms that turned briefly into sleet. It might have settled in some areas, but in the city it melted like wax on a hot-plate. The hospital visits were increasingly difficult. Daniel seemed threatened by the prospect of leaving. When he talked to Peter he looked past him; both literally and in what he said. 'I want to move north... Contact some old friends, start again.' These remarks never sounded like plans, more like the details on a passport.

As usual, on the twentieth day of the month Peter's landlord came round for the rent cheque. Peter explained that he was waiting for the DSS to pay Daniel's share of the rent, while he was in hospital and unemployed. The landlord was a confident young man who lived in Solihull; he was wearing a pale grey suit and a gold signet ring. He gave Peter a rather unfriendly smile. 'I know everybody's hard up at Christmas,' he said. 'It's difficult for me as well. If I don't get the money into the building society by the end of the year I'll have to start breaking into capital, which I don't like to do. Maybe you should think about moving. I'll come back early in the new year and we'll see if the situation has improved.' He folded Peter's cheque in the palm of his hand like a love letter. 'Hope you have a good Christmas.'

When he'd gone, Peter felt unable to stay in the flat. He walked up towards the High Street, past a series of dark three-storey houses that were divided into tenements. From one house alone, you could make enough income to live on. And if you owned half a street... It was frightening, when you thought about it in that way. To have a good job, a career, a decent wage; that was one thing. But just to have cash that multiplied itself like a sack of worms... Peter imagined money breeding in the dark. Whitish banknotes spilling from chests, fluttering onto the dusty floor of a sealed vault. He couldn't face the evening on his own. The bus going into town seemed to take forever, wandering through the back streets of a trading estate between Balsall Heath and Deritend: tall warehouses and office blocks, their upper windows all smashed, their lower windows dark behind wire grids. Nearer town, coloured bulbs were strung out on cables above the roadway.

Starlings, a bar just off New Street, was usually dead in midweek. But Christmas brought everyone out. The DJ was playing a selection of new chart records, as well as his standard list of tracks. Twenty or so people jostled on the tiny dance floor. Red and gold lights were scattered on the walls, though the velvet-covered sofas at the back were in virtual darkness. Couples embraced there, out of sight, each holding the other like a shield. Young people, many of them students, were clustered around the tables. A few solitary figures hung on the edge of the dance floor, waiting. This was predominantly a women's bar; though again, that was less true at Christmas. Men were less sociable than women, more dependent on bars for human contact.

There was nobody in sight that Peter knew well enough to have a conversation with. He'd been out of touch for too long. He drifted briefly between the tables, feeling like a gatecrasher at a teenage party. It was hard to distinguish between male and female faces in the half-light. There was an hour left until closing time; Peter began drinking fast, trying to dissolve the chill that was growing in his mind. As he stood at the bar, a man he didn't recognise got up and approached him cautiously. He was in his forties, balding, with very pale skin and worried eyes. He glanced down at Peter's nearly empty glass.

'Want a drink, son?'

Peter shook his head. 'No thanks, I'm fine.'

The stranger propped his elbows on the bar. His hands were trembling. 'Go on, it's Christmas. Let me get you a drink. Please. What do you want?'

'Half a lager, thanks.' Peter felt a hollow ache in his gut that came from having already drunk too much, too quickly. Behind him, the dancing had slowed to the last few quiet numbers; couples were stumbling in the dark square of the floor, their movements limited by contact. The man passed him a drink. 'Thank you.'

The other smiled at him. 'No problem. I get lonely at Christmas. Need a drink. And someone to talk to.'

'Doesn't everyone?' Peter gulped his drink. Suddenly he felt too tired to move.

'I really like you.'

'You don't know me.' Christ, the guy must be drunk to make an advance that quick, without encouragement. Perhaps he was used to a different situation.

'Do you want to come back to mine?' He didn't seem to hear anything Peter said. The record ended and the dancers stood in silence, waiting for the lights to go up.

'No, I'm sorry.' He was on the point of losing his temper. But there was no real anger in him, only a deepening sense of unease. 'I can't.'

'Please. It's Christmas. You won't regret it. I'll be gentle, I promise. You needn't be afraid.'

'Look, I'm sorry. I have to go.'

'What, back to mine?'

'No.' Peter stood up and put his coat on, then walked out into the alley. Halfway down to New Street, his unease caught up with him and he leaned against the wall, shaking. The alley was paved with bricks, like another wall. It was starting to rain. But his face wasn't a window. Because he couldn't see the rain, it didn't seem real. On the way home, a song that the DJ in Starlings had played echoed in his head, not fading but getting louder with each repetition. Back in the flat, he sat in darkness on the bed, drinking whisky mixed with water until he lost consciousness. The next morning, he phoned in sick, then got up late and went to visit Daniel in the hospital.

That weekend, the last before Christmas, Peter got his things sorted out and packed ready for the trip to Lincoln. The process left him feeling desperate for a drink and a chat. Starlings, he knew, would be too crowded and hot to endure. And if he went to a nightclub, the atmosphere and his own feelings would more than likely drive him into someone else's bed. It had happened once already. And he wanted to go home with a clearer mind than that. He had to think, not let his thoughts just happen. Drink helped. Sex helped. But they didn't touch whatever it was displaced you from your own life, took away your sense of direction, so that you had nothing left for dealing with the future except a handful of reflexes that could belong to anyone.

He stretched out on the bed, trying to earth his thoughts. It wasn't his fault; nobody had said it was. Anyway, Daniel was all right now. 'Guilt never helps anybody. Ian's more to blame.' Daniel would have gone back to his parents, but Ian had persuaded them not to let him move in. Peter remembered how Daniel had looked when Peter had come home from work and found him lying here, like this. He'd taken a bottle of sleeping pills. The General Hospital had transferred him to a psychiatric ward, more because of Daniel's attack on his brother than because of the suicide attempt. That was eight weeks ago. But he was a voluntary patient, unless anything worse happened. 'You could leave there any time. But you don't know what's going to happen after. Nor do I. We're both doing the same thing. Playing dead.'

Speaking it out loud helped. But telling it, even fragments and versions of it, made it less real, as though it were a story from a newspaper. Peter sat in the dark living room, playing records and tapes, until nothing remained clear to him. Except the unfamiliar truth. Not because he loved Daniel, not any more. He wished he could write songs, or paint, or even play an instrument. Without a medium like that, there was no such thing as confession. There was only talk.

Peter met Daniel outside the hospital, at noon on the thirtieth of December. It was a bright day; the sun flickered coldly behind streaks of cloud. On the way home, they talked about the news, which Daniel had been following on TV. 'It feels like mythology,' he was saying. 'Tyrants overthrown, walls broken down, end of the Cold War. So little has really changed, but everyone's stoned on the future. You wait and see. It must have felt a bit like this in the late sixties.' Peter nodded, agreeing. Britain's contribution to the new international spirit seemed to be captured in the British National Party's stickers on the bus shelter. And the prime minister's remark that she would be happy to lead a united Europe. He quoted that to Daniel, who laughed. 'Playground mentality. It's funny how people never leave childhood. They call it instinct, but it's not.'

When they got back to the flat, the conversation faded out. Daniel walked from room to room as though seeing the place for the first time. Then he started unpacking his suitcase. The plan was that he would stay over two nights, then go back on New Year's Day. All being well, he'd be out for good a few days after that. He didn't say anything about the hospital, or his state of mind. Peter didn't ask anything. Suddenly, it was impossible to forget things that, for weeks, he'd found difficult to remember. What it had been like just before Daniel's breakdown: the surreal arguments; the days and nights without talking; how tension had seemed to distort the space of the flat. Daniel was quiet, communicating mostly through glances that seemed either scared or resentful. The two avoided contact. When Daniel kissed him unexpectedly, late in the afternoon, Peter flinched and drew back. 'It's all right,' Daniel said. 'You're quite safe. I left the hockey mask and the meat cleaver back in occupational therapy.' Peter felt more comfortable watching Daniel tune his guitar, adjusting the tension in each string with a patience he'd never had in speech. Each harsh note stubbed itself out on the walls, almost echoing.

They shared a bottle of wine with dinner, and Daniel started to relax. He phoned a few friends and caught up with their news, said he hoped to see them before long. Later in the evening, Daniel and Peter sat together on the couch and listened to music. The only light in the room came from the gas fire, which warmed a cell of air just in front of it. Their bodies shadowed the heat just as effectively as they did the light.

Peter could make out only a sketch of Daniel; his eyes and mouth were dark holes. He was thinner than Peter remembered him. Behind them, the record player pounded out damage and atonement. It made the room seem much bigger than it was. They undressed each other and made love, for the first time since October. It took a long time; they were unused to each other. Daniel didn't seem to respond or be influenced by touch in the same way as before. Nothing had really been lost, but they had both changed.

It was after midnight when Daniel got up and started to dress. Peter reached up and caught his arm. 'Where you going?'

'A walk. I can't go to bed yet. Need some fresh air.' He fumbled for his clothes in the darkness. 'Will you come with me? Please?'

'Sure.' Peter walked across to the window and pressed his hands to the damp glass, then rubbed his face. He looked at Daniel and laughed. 'You're wearing my shirt.'

Daniel looked down. 'So I am. Does it matter?'

'No.' They put their coats on and walked down the uncarpeted stairway to the front door. Outside, the road was empty, frosted with light. Houses were as displaced and still as exhibits in a museum gallery. Daniel walked fast; he seemed on edge. Peter struggled to keep up with him. 'Where are we going?'

'The park,' Daniel said. That was at the northern end of the High Street, behind a line of poplar trees like giant railings. A few sodium lamps marked out the pathways through several acres of grass, overgrown shrubbery and woodland. Peter and Daniel walked together down a gravel footpath that soon became nearly invisible. Trees looked vast and distorted overhead. The sky was clear, but there was no moon. Peter recognised the three stars in Orion's belt. It would be brighter here if the sky were clouded over, reflecting back the light from the city. The path ended at a shelter which was flaky with old paint.

'Can we stop a minute?' Peter said. 'I'm getting tired.' His muscles ached, and the cold made him want to curl up and hide his face. They sat down on the far side of the shelter, leaning back against concrete. Daniel stared into the unlit mass of trees and bushes ahead of them. Looking, Peter could see a dim series of lines imposed on his view. Slowly, as his eyes adjusted, he could make out the criss-cross pattern of a wire fence. He leaned his head on Daniel's shoulder, tilting one ear when Daniel spoke to him.

'I've been here many times,' the other said quietly. 'Late at night, when I couldn't face staying in with you. You'd be watching TV or reading, and I'd come out here and walk around. Summer nights, you see a lot of men down here, just waiting. It's strange. After a while I could recognise people. I've never seen them anywhere else. Sometimes I'd say hello. But that was all. I didn't want anyone. I just wanted to be alone.' He gripped Peter's shoulder and pulled him closer. 'It was never as cold as this. I'm glad you're here.' Daniel's face was cold to touch. His words left brief trails of vapour, dissolving back into silence. Peter felt unable to move or think.

Some time later, the back of his head tapped the concrete wall. His eyes opened on a darkness that was almost complete. Daniel had gone. Christ, how long had he been asleep? It was too dark to read his watch. Peter struggled to his feet and stood reaching forward, unbalanced. Perhaps Daniel had got cramp, or felt cold, or needed to piss. He walked round the shelter a few times, but nothing moved. He waited another ten minutes or so, then began to retrace his steps along the footpath. But without a guide, he wasn't sure if this was even the same route. What if Daniel had been mugged? Questions tangled in his mind as he walked through a network of crossed paths. Had Daniel gone home? That was most likely, assuming he still had his key. But perhaps he'd just taken off somewhere, and Peter might never see him or hear from him again. He walked faster, using rage to help him see, shouting Daniel's name against the wall of absence. He circled the park once, then crossed through the middle. He came to the gateway at the corner of the main road and stood looking at the black strip of flower bed, the line of poplar trees at the park's boundary. Then he walked on, slowly, to the High Street.

The roads were empty, except for a few vagrants stirring in doorways and bus shelters. Peter had to force himself to keep moving; the pavement seemed to drain energy from him. He had nothing but stone to hold onto. Finally, he reached a dark house and turned the key in the front door. Footsteps sounded behind him, running. He turned. 'Daniel!' The other caught up, stopped. 'Christ, where have you been?' Peter seized his arm, pulled him close. 'Where were you? I've been looking for you for about an hour!'

'I know.' Daniel's face was impenetrable.

'Where have you been?'

'I was following you. You went all the way round the park, clockwise, then back through the middle. You waited near the gate, then left.' The front door was open. Peter reached inside, pressed the light switch. They stood in the hall, shivering.

'But why?'

'To show you how it feels.'

The timeswitch went off. They climbed the stairs in darkness, holding onto each other, Daniel leading the way.

THICKER THAN WATER

Paul had never seen any of the canal people, but he knew all about them. Everyone knew. The way Kevin had worded it, the assignment didn't require him to find anything out. 'Go and have a look. Get a feel for the district. It might give you some ideas for a feature... What we need, Paul, is a serious campaign. Rumours are not enough. The city needs a real answer to this problem.' Of course, Kevin would never tell him to make things up. That way, he couldn't be held responsible for what the *Messenger* printed; or its effects. Paul didn't know if the *Messenger*'s editor was capable of feeling guilty. He only knew that guilt made you lie to yourself, as well as to others.

The afternoon dragged, while Paul browsed through the archive office's local press cuttings on 'the problem'. It was too hot to do much active work; and there was no fan in the archive office, which smelt of old paper. There were reports, going back five or ten years, about the vagrant communities around Dudley and West Bromwich. One article said they were gypsies; another said they were just ordinary sub-citizens on the run from the authorities. They drifted up from the South and got stuck here. Paul didn't like the word 'sub-citizen'; it reminded him of 'sub-editor', which was his job most of the time. He preferred to use the old-fashioned words like scum, dropout or criminal.

Even from the early years, there were stories about break-ins and thefts from shops and warehouses in these districts. Mostly food and clothes, rather than things to be resold. Lately, of course, the accusations were more serious. But the whole situation had changed. Groups of squatters were occupying the derelict offices and tenement buildings, driving out the legitimate community. They weren't canal people any more, though the name had stuck. The *Messenger* had carried a story about disappeared babies and small children. Kevin wasn't a fool. He'd remarked to Paul that when babies went missing in bad areas, especially when the parents were young, it was easier to blame the gypsies than to investigate. This summer, with the heat and the water shortages, disease was spreading in the unsafe areas. Most local people hoped it would wipe out the vagrants before they contaminated the city.

The air in the archive office grew hotter as the afternoon progressed and the sun drew level with the windows. Paul's vision blurred as his contact lenses began to swell up; rubbing his eyes got dust onto the surfaces, and he couldn't blink it away He gave up reading and let the anger in his mind edit and stress the thoughts. A big fly, droning at the window, had the same effect. When it settled within Paul's reach, he smeared it with the palm of his hand. At once, he made for the toilets and washed his hands with a liquid soap that had the consistency of saliva. The sound of water running in the basin made him pause, briefly unable to move. He didn't know why, and he felt guilty about wasting tap water. After that, he filed away the newspaper cuttings and left early.

When he got home, Carol was in a bad mood. Their elder daughter, Dawn, had been off school with an attack of dysentery. Paul went up to see her, but she was asleep in a darkened room. 'I want to talk to you after dinner,' Carol said. They ate in a fatigued silence; even Stella, their younger daughter, was unusually quiet. Dawn stayed in her room. After dinner, Paul watched the news on three channels in succession. The living room was still full of sunlight; it felt wrong this late. The fly's blood was a streak across his thoughts. He wondered why it was paler than human blood. The local news on the independent channel included a report on the new science and technology exhibition centre at Monkspath. Someone from the city council described it as part of this year's major initiative to brighten up the region's image.

Paul got up and went into the kitchen, where he poured himself a large gin. From habit, he filled up the glass with ice; then he wished he'd left it neat. He was still staring at the glass when Carol found him. 'Paul,' she said. 'I found this with your clothes.' It was a page from a local newspaper, not the *Messenger*; she had to unfold it several times. Paul blinked at it and restrained himself from drinking.

'Yeh,' he said. 'Story I covered. But they never used it. This is someone else's write-up, for the *Express and Star*.'

'What a tragic business. Was it someone you knew?'

Paul shook his head. 'No, I just investigated it. Didn't find out any more than this reporter. Happens all the time, you know. Unwanted pregnancies, botched abortions, even this.' He swallowed his gin before too much of the ice could melt into it.

Carol shrugged. 'Funny thing to keep.' She folded up the page, then absent-mindedly tore it into four pieces. 'Sorry, did you want it?'

Paul shook his head again. He suppressed the impulse to shout *Fuck, what did you do that for?* 'How's Dawn?' he asked as the gin started to blacken his nerves. He felt like a photograph left too long in developing fluid.

'Shitting and vomiting,' Carol said. 'But nothing dangerous, no blood. The doctor says she'll be okay in three or four days. She needs to rest as much as possible. Paul, I found something else. In an envelope, in your desk. I've thrown them away.'

'What were you looking there for?'

'Paul... You don't use condoms with me. On the rare occasions that we have sex, you don't use them. Who are they for?'

'Keep your voice down. Stella will hear you.' Paul finished his drink. Carol was still staring at him. 'All right,' he said. 'I fuck the office boy in my lunch breaks.'

'Was it that Alison Simmons?'

'And coffee breaks.'

'Did you forget once? Was that why—'

'Shut your face.' Paul stood up. With one hand, he mimed the closing of a mouth. Then he stared at his fist, remembering the fly and its thin blood. Thinner than water. He felt himself seize up. It never happened, he told himself.

Only on the surface, the acts, the facts, the story. It was never real inside me.

Was it real inside her? 'Leave me alone,' he said quietly. Carol went upstairs. She was good like that sometimes. Paul looked around the kitchen. The wall was flecked with damp; it needed repainting. Perhaps he'd do it soon, and show he was a good family man. Only squatters let the places they lived in fall apart. It was growing dark outside. Paul carried on drinking. He heard Carol putting Stella to bed, heard Dawn saying goodnight. He'd seen her upstairs an hour before, heading for the toilet. She looked pale and dark-eyed, like a figure from a Munch engraving.

When Paul went up to bed, the house was still. Carol was waiting for him. 'Sorry,' he said, as if that could atone for all past, present and future offences. In the dark, she tried to caress him. 'Sorry,' he said again, this time meaning: *It's the drink.* They both knew it wasn't only the gin. He'd been impotent with Carol ever since... well, since Alison died. He knew Carol would have connected the times when she saw the newspaper cutting. She always kept diaries and calendars. Why did she try to make love to him even when they'd had a row? Because she had no other source of comfort, Paul thought; he felt paralysed with guilt. Carol lay still, holding him tight against her. He tried to will some of his alcoholic calm into her taut muscles. After a few minutes, she turned over and went to sleep, curled inward on herself.

The next morning, Paul visited the canal district for the first time. It was another hot, bright day; the city centre was choked with traffic. Young army recruits hung around the shopping precincts, their faces marked by the sun with a look of perpetual embarrassment. The shop windows were like dusty mirrors. Days like this numbed your vision, so you couldn't see properly in the shade. Paul considered going into the office to catch up with some routine subbing and admin work for next Sunday's issue of the *Messenger*. But instead, he caught the bus out towards West Bromwich. It took him past the house on the Hagley Road where Alison had lived. Further north, Smethwick was a grey chessboard of terraces and factory walls, like an open-plan prison. From a hilltop, Paul could see the glint of water in the reservoir's drying socket.

What was he looking for? Where he got off the bus, the street was empty. He walked through a circular shopping precinct where only a few small offices were open. The shops themselves were boarded up, the boards sprayed with messages that overlaid each other into meaninglessness, like voices in a crowded place. This place felt crowded even though nobody was around. In the middle of the precinct, a hot-food kiosk had been literally plated with armour. On three sides, tower blocks reared up against the sky; their balconies overlooked the courtyard where Paul was standing. Each storey was about eight feet deep. Looking upward, he had a terrible sense of the ground being hollow.

Further away from the main road, the streets were lined with factory walls; rusty steel hooks and coils of barbed wire protected the interior. One large building had been demolished, leaving only a roofless square of grey wall around a salvage dump. The unreal blue of the sky framed each building. Then, suddenly, he was walking past a series of little housing projects, each one a flattened U-shape around a gravel courtyard. They couldn't date back any further than the 1990s, but already their model village effect was threadbare. Most of the flats were untenanted; in some cases, blankets or pieces of tarpaulin were nailed across the window frames. Doorways were padlocked and chained, but not sealed up. The courtyards and the entry passages between buildings were littered with black plastic bags and crates full of refuse. A few rusty shells of cars perched in driveways, without wheels. On a hilltop, a children's playground contained various elaborate climbing frames, but no children.

Paul walked on for some time before he saw anyone. It was too hot for activity. The older part of the district was less visibly derelict than the estates; perhaps the occupants were harder to dislodge. Tower blocks, crusted with scaffolding like insects shedding their skins, broke up the pattern of terraced houses. Rubbish was everywhere – in gutters, beside doorsteps, blocking the entries to the alleyways – but it was too dry to smell really bad. A frail-looking dog clawed slowly at a heap of refuse bags; a few gnats flickered above the animal's head like a heat-haze. Beyond, Paul could see a man crouching in the alley. At the sight of him, the other backed away and was lost in the shadows. Paul had a momentary sensation of being the hunter. Reporters were supposed to be witnesses; but forget that for the time being. If he didn't do something, there might not be much to witness.

The alley was empty. They always kept themselves hidden. That was how they got away with it. At the far end, the boarding of windows in the terraced houses suggested occupation: it had been done clumsily, with odd pieces of broken plank. Pieces of black cloth were nailed to several of the boards, like a torn flag. It was evidently some kind of sub-community effort. The houses were about ten feet wide; Paul wondered who could have lived there in the first place. A gap between two houses looked like another alley, but turned out to be the bridge over a canal. Even from this distance, the water stank. Gnats made the warm air shiver. Paul bit his lip. If he vomited here, what could he rinse his mouth with? He watched a crow flap up from underneath the bridge, carrying a piece of refuse in its beak. Water dripped across the bright pavement. Within minutes, as Paul stared at the road, the splashes dried to faint red smears.

When Paul was six years old, his parents had taken him to the Welsh coast for a fortnight in the summer. That was when he'd started learning to swim. One of the days, they were walking inland across the fields. Paul had seen a sheep fence made of barbed wire, with tufts of wool hanging from it. Some of the wool was red. His mother had said it was the dye that farmers used to mark their own sheep. She'd also told him that taking communion in church meant drinking the blood of Christ. Paul stared at the sky. The sky stared back at him. It must be a stray dog in the canal. There were packs of dogs roaming around down there. It wasn't courage that made him find the stone steps at the side of the bridge. It was something he didn't have a name for.

The walls of the bridge were crusted with whitish deposits of lime. The water level was several feet below the towpath. Heaped in the water, not floating but piled on top of each other, were at least twenty human bodies. Some of them were too small to be adult. Though discoloured and slightly swollen with water, they could not have been there long. Birds or rats had torn pieces off them, but Paul could see the marks of rifle bullets in their heads and bodies. Beyond the bridge, trails of blood had dried and blackened like tar. The only sound Paul could hear was the droning of flies, the same sound that had been in his head for weeks.

———————

It wasn't water flowing across his face. It was light. Paul woke up in a painful shudder that meant he'd lost whatever he'd been dreaming. He forced his eyes to stay open. The edges of red clouds were bleached by the sun. He must have passed out last night and forgotten to shut the curtains. He was sleeping in the spare bedroom now, which was Carol's idea but suited him okay. Stella was with Carol, and Dawn was still recovering. But they were not foremost in Paul's thoughts at the moment. He had an hour before he needed to go into work. It was Friday, the third day since his visit to the canal district.

Kevin's reaction had upset him, but he was getting used to it now. The *Messenger*'s editor had listened to Paul's story in silence, then told him to get on with the sub-editing for the next issue. 'Remember what I said, Paul? The city needs an answer to this problem. If the army boys are sorting it out in their own way, all well and good.' He took a deep breath and looked straight at Paul, straight through the back of his head at the photographs and documents on the far wall. You have to consider the effect of what gets printed. It's for the benefit of the community. The real people of the city.'

Paul nodded and stood up; Kevin saw his hands shake. 'Don't go back there,' he said. 'And get your drinking under control, unless you want to end up on the street.' It didn't matter now, Paul realised. Human life was only the surface of things. As always in a crisis, faith comforted him and helped him to accept the way things had to be. With a strange sense of detachment, he wondered about the future: the lives of his children, his grandchildren. What memories would Dawn and Stella have of him? For a moment he felt cold. They'd heard him and Carol screaming at each other in the night, so many times. It was unbelievable, the things they'd come out with. But his parents had been just the same. Had that affected him?

Still feeling unreal, he got up to go to the bathroom. The frosted glass above the washbasin trapped a layer of pinkish light, like the skin of an angel. He ran lukewarm water into the basin, while his reflection in the mirror ignored him. The inside of his mouth was coated with the taste of alcohol; he could feel it in his gut, cold like silver. He listened to the sound of his own breathing. He needed to piss, but he'd have to wait until his prick went down. What had he been dreaming about? Paul waited for a long time before touching the water in the basin. He was afraid to break its surface. In the end he washed with his eyes shut, and cut himself shaving.

As he dressed and left for work, Paul kept thinking of Alison. She wasn't the first mistress he'd had, but she was the first who'd threatened his marriage. For Paul, these affairs were a kind of escape. He didn't allow them to become real. It was the sense of danger that turned him on. He suspected that, without Carol to go back to, he wouldn't have bothered with any of them. Alison had seemed just his type. She was young and easily controlled, and she drank even more than Paul did. He saw her once or twice a week, always parking his car some distance from the house where she lodged.

It had gone on for nearly a year. There was something in Alison he'd never found before, and couldn't put into words. She came from the coast – the Isle of Wight – and city life was strange to her. She sometimes talked about swimming in the sea, the freedom and wildness of it. That had been the only good thing about her childhood. She'd left home at fifteen, gone to London, then drifted up into the Midlands like so many others. Her room was full of shells and flowers and old records; having developed a catlike adaptation to confined spaces, she didn't like to go out. She had a good voice, but Paul didn't like to hear her sing; it frightened him, for some reason. What did it mean to want what you were most afraid of? Or to fear what you most wanted?

He'd left Alison when she'd refused to have an abortion. It wouldn't have been the first time for her, so Paul had felt justified in taking a firm stand. She'd asked him to divorce Carol, and he'd explained to her that divorce was wrong, and abandoning your family was more so. He shouldn't even have had to explain these things to Alison. She'd called him a two-faced bastard, and that had been the end of it. He'd stopped calling on her, and was relieved when she didn't try to find him. Months later he'd come across the story of her death, while flicking through a day-old copy of a rival newspaper on the bus. Alison's landlord had broken her door down and found her dead from an overdose of sleeping pills. She was six months pregnant. The foetus inside her had died at the same time.

This morning, Paul felt as though he were committed to her. He felt displaced from his former life. Was that because of the trouble in his marriage, or the trouble in his job? Or the drink, which was having the same effect on both? Getting drunk was a way of remembering Alison, as well as of returning to his own childhood. Of course, getting drunk didn't make you like a child; it just made you feel that you were. The bus into town was packed with fresh-faced office workers, just the wrong side of a nine o'clock start. He told himself he'd have the car back soon. It was only a three-month ban: clumsy driving, slightly over the limit; nobody had been hurt.

The brilliant sunlight shadowed him from New Street to the *Messenger*'s offices in Hockley. It glittered from car roofs and scaffolding and broken glass. The roadway between Snow Hill and the old Hockley flyover was all elevated above ground level. If you looked at the advertisement boards, you could forget where you were.

Inside his office, Paul felt more secure. His computer terminal was as reassuring as a piano, and much quieter. He edited on-screen, not bothering to mark corrections on a printout beforehand. The added eyestrain was compensated by the sense of potency. Suddenly he wished his own life story were on the screen. Then every morning, he could retrieve himself; correct himself; justify himself; save himself. The pun reminded him of something he couldn't quite bring to mind. There was the usual scattering of civic events to deal with. Another story about the new science exhibition centre; and one about the new sports complex, designed with half an eye on some future Olympic Games. A handful of robbery, violence and accident stories; still nothing about the canal district.

He spoke to Kevin at lunchtime. The editor was looking tense and on edge, which struck Paul as a good sign. 'Are you still ignoring what happened?' he asked. On a better day, Kevin might have pretended not to understand him. But he stared hard at Paul, then shook his head.

'The situation seems to be under control,' he said. 'We don't want to stir up public interest in the area. Or innocent people will get hurt… It's not as though people don't know what's going on. But it's in the sub-citizens' interests to keep things quiet. Preserve calm. Most of them will be transported out of the districts where these communities are. Dispersed or jailed. The only alternative is what you saw. It's got to happen, one way or the other.' He walked away before Paul could interpret the unease in his face.

For the next hour, Paul sat in the canteen and watched the reporters and ad men and typists come and go. Who could he talk to that might understand? The faces of the young men reminded him of the army recruits he'd seen in the city centre on Tuesday. It was still easy for him to see the young as perfect versions, originals of which he was a defective offprint. But he knew from experience, they were bastards in embryo. Their apparent perfection was just immaturity. He'd never trusted men. Or women. Was that because he didn't trust himself? He thought about Carol, and knew he'd have to patch things up this weekend. The decision gave him no comfort.

Quite suddenly, with no external jog to his memory, he knew what the pun about saving himself had reminded him of. It was a line of poetry – some Irish poet from the late twentieth century that his mother had liked. Seamus Heaney, that was it:

Where to be saved you only must save face
And whatever you say, you say nothing.

In the afternoon, Paul started to fall asleep at his desk. The pile of typescripts under his hands made him dream about a bundle of newspaper. Three old women were sitting in a brick-walled alley somewhere beyond reach of the sun: they were passing the bundle back and forth between them. Each tore away a layer and passed on the rest of it, like a party game. Paul could still hear the clicking of printers from the office, but he refused to open his eyes. There was nothing inside the bundle, unless it was too dry and shrunken to tell apart from the last twisted-up pages, grey with newsprint. The wrinkled hands of the old women were covered with stories. Paul woke with a shock that felt like a magnesium flare in his head. He arranged the sheets on his desk into a logical order, scrambled them and rearranged them. How long could it be before someone noticed he'd done nothing?

Somehow he got through the bulk of work on his desk, half-aware of errors he was letting through or even creating. What did anyone care? If they were comfortable with lies, it was absurd for them to worry about spelling and punctuation. He could always give it a final check tomorrow morning. At five o'clock Paul unplugged his computer. Instead of catching the bus into town, he walked into the nearest pub. The beer was tepid and had a stiff head he could have shaved with. He drank three pints in half an hour. When he went to piss, the water streaming down the sides of the urinal paralysed him; he couldn't look away.

The bus that took him to the canal district went by a different route from the one he'd caught on Tuesday. Paul didn't recognise the streets, until he saw the elevated concrete circle of the shopping precinct, with the blocks of flats built around its edge. He got off and stood holding onto the white wall that fronted the expressway, telling himself the buildings weren't really tilted. A white-haired alcoholic in a blue anorak knelt on the pavement, singing to himself. In the precinct, an Alsatian was trying to push through the jagged gap a brick had left in a shop window. Paul could hear pieces of glass fall and smash as the dog broke through. There was nobody else in sight, and no traffic on the road.

It took Paul a long time to find the canal bridge among the terraces, and even then he wasn't sure it was the same one. The canal was stagnant, and shapeless hulks of furniture or tree branches littered its surface; but there was no trace of what he'd seen three days before. He made his way cautiously along the canal towpath towards the next bridge. The buildings overhead became taller, factories rather than houses. He had an overwhelming sense of neglect and disuse – of an old network whose purpose was hardly remembered, submerged beneath the new roads and concrete walkways. An old word for canal was *cut*, he'd read somewhere. It was supposed to be a part of local dialect. The cut; the missing frame; the part of the story condemned to silence.

An hour later, he still hadn't found any evidence of either life or death along the canal. Soon he'd have to give up and find his way back to the city centre. But he was completely lost now. There were no streets within sight of the towpath: only a blank factory wall, a scrapyard, a grassy embankment. Some goods carriages stood empty on a rusty track. The sun was low in the sky ahead, its reddish beams dividing the close air into layers. Paul's eyes were starting to sting and blur. Even when he thought his inability to cry would make him go blind, there was nothing he could do. The accumulated dirt on the walls and stone bridges seemed to bring the night closer. Not far ahead, the view disappeared into the mouth of a tunnel. Perhaps he could rest in there, shielded from the glare of the sun. But he was still in the open air when the tunnel bit him.

Pain turned the world inside-out. There was stone inside him, and flesh on the path. He was staring down into a cloudless sky, at the black afterimage of the sun. Why did he have to keep waking up like this? Then he looked at himself and thought: *Jesus wept*. It was some kind of wire snare, a net with hooks. Had he walked into a tripwire? The pain was receding now; it was only a background noise. Lifting himself on one arm, he realised the snare had almost missed him. Hooks had scored his chest and belly on the left side, almost removing his shirt. More hooks were embedded in his left arm; but he couldn't feel them.

Fucking bastards. Was it a gypsy trap for stray dogs? Or an army trap for vagrants? Very slowly, Paul sat up and looked around him. There was nobody within sight. In the tunnel, something dark was floating on the water; a canal barge, he realised, moored to the bank. He looked up at the buildings above the towpath. They might be houses, but he couldn't see them properly. *Fuck it*. He called out 'Help': the sound was absurdly thin, a child's voice. One by one, he detached the remaining hooks from the flesh of his arm.

There might be someone aboard the barge. Paul walked under the bridge, his arms locked together in a cradle of whole and injured flesh. The feeling was gone from the left side of his body. Flanking the tunnel on either side was a series of brick-lined alcoves that reminded him of a museum gallery. There were images on the walls, crusts of lichen or chemical waste that absorbed moisture from the air. The barge seemed to be pulling slowly away from him. As he got closer to it, he could see that the black wood of its hull was rotten and streaked with lime. Someone was sitting on its roof, facing him; so still, he thought she must be dead. Then she leaned forward and touched his face. The fingers were soft and cool. Her other arm was holding a child, pressed close to her, its head in the hollow of her throat. The child too was facing him. It had no mouth.

Someone moved behind him. Paul turned and saw thin figures emerging from the alcoves, on both sides of the tunnel. One of the canal people stepped closer and touched Paul's injured arm. It was still bleeding, but the fluid that ran from it wasn't blood. Paul could see the blue of his own tattered shirt; and flowing from the wounds in his arm, a dirty water that smelt like the canal. The man behind him ripped the sleeve from his own shirt, then tied it around Paul's arm. The flow stopped, but the numbness remained. Paul looked back at the face of the child. Other people were drawing closer around him. He wanted to tell them that he didn't need to be rescued, that this was where he belonged. But he couldn't speak. They seemed to understand in any case. Some of them helped him to climb aboard the barge. When the barge started to move, Paul realised the sunlight had deceived him. This wasn't a tunnel, nor, strictly speaking, a canal.

BRANDED

The sound of gravel against her window woke her around three in the morning. It was Matthew, of course. Moving lightly, she went downstairs and unlocked the back door. The chilly September night smelt of rain and dead leaves. In the kitchen, Matthew took off his shoes. He looked pale and scared. Lisa unzipped his jacket and pulled him against her, kissing him slowly. 'It's all right,' she whispered. 'You're safe here.' But the words meant nothing. She took his hand and led him carefully up the stairs to her room. The sleeve of his jacket was damp; he'd splashed petrol on it.

The night was dead quiet: no traffic, no sirens, no voices. Only the distant whirring of a police helicopter. Matthew stretched out on her bed and lay still. He was both tense and exhausted. Lisa offered him a can of Lilt. 'Thanks.' Still half dressed, she lay down beside him, her head on his arm. 'There'll be hell to pay tomorrow,' she heard him whisper. It was like someone miming to a voice a long way off. 'I'll have to go back. I couldn't last on the streets. I've seen what that's like. But you wouldn't believe the shit they give you for stopping out. Cunts.' Lisa had been fostered a couple of years back. Matthew was still in care. They'd been friends since Lisa had come to Birmingham, three years before that. Puberty hadn't changed him much. But he was changing now.

'It's good to see you,' he said gently. 'I felt so alone tonight.' She gripped his hand. The nails were bitten ragged; there were red scratches across the knuckles. 'I hit a wall,' he said. Lisa sat up, took a roll of Elastoplast from her bedside cabinet and covered the damaged area. He leaned towards her; his eyes were bloodshot. As they kissed, he gripped her arms and pulled her down beside him. They undressed each other and made love as quietly as possible. Matthew held her so close, every part of himself pressed against her, that she felt joined to him. They hardly needed to move. Long ago, she'd realised that his intensity was a way of overcoming a fear of contact. The first time they'd slept together, they'd both been fourteen. He'd been a virgin.

Afterwards, Matthew was still tense. She resigned herself to sleepwalking through the next day at school. 'What happened tonight?' she whispered. He shook his head and looked away. The sweat on his back glistened like molten wax. She touched it and felt him flinch involuntarily. His sweat should be red, she thought. Probably he'd burned something down. A rubbish dump, a car in a scrapyard, maybe a derelict house. Or... The back of his head muttered. She leaned over him. 'You what?'

He pressed his mouth to her ear. 'If I don't tell you, then you don't know. You shouldn't have to keep secrets.' Lisa didn't know what to say. She'd never shop him. He was Matthew. He hadn't killed anyone. Whatever people told you to believe, there were some kinds of loyalty you didn't forget. Otherwise you became dead inside. Like a security camera, observing but not *there*. She knew Matthew trusted her; it made her feel lost.

'Do you mind if I smoke?' Matthew shook his head. Lisa reached under the bed for a packet of Marlboros, lit one and inhaled deeply. Fibres of shadow dissolved above her face. She began to calm down. Matthew gazed at her uneasily through the smoke. His eyes followed the tip of her cigarette. 'Are you all right?' she said.

He bit his lip. 'Yeah. My mouth feels dead.' She leant over to kiss him; his lips didn't respond. The sweat on his face was cold. 'You know why I don't smoke?' he said. 'It tastes of nothing.' Lisa crushed her cigarette against the wall and let it drop. Then she pulled the duvet over them both. Matthew began to shake when she embraced him. She lay still and let him press his face against her neck. After a while she felt his tears on her skin, warm and silent.

It had to be now. While he wasn't either awake or asleep. Cautiously, Lisa ran one hand down his side, from the ribcage to the hip. From there, the line of scars crossed his thigh and ran down the inside to his calf. It was the same on the other side. Small circular marks, like bullet holes. They were at least ten years old, she knew. In poor light they made him look like a doll. Like someone had cut him lengthways, filled him with explosive and then stitched him up again. Lisa thought of sirens and the red eyes of fire engines in the night. What difference could touching make? Her hand moved up to his neck, stroking his cropped dark hair. Soon he was asleep.

'Lisa.' He was standing by the bed, dressed. In the grey light of early morning, his face was like a newspaper photo. 'I have to go. Before she wakes up.' He meant Lisa's adoptive mother, whose husband was away working on a North Sea oil rig. Having Lisa around helped her to feel secure. It was nearly six o'clock. Lisa put on her school clothes and led Matthew downstairs to the kitchen, where his shoes were. From the weight of his body, she knew he could have done with more sleep. 'Do you need some money?' she whispered.

He shook his head. 'I wouldn't mind some food, though.' Lisa searched quickly, found him two packets of biscuits and a bar of Galaxy chocolate. 'Thanks. For everything.' Once again, she couldn't speak. Instead of unlocking the back door, she led him through the house to the front door and closed it quietly behind them. They walked through a little shopping precinct where half the shops were boarded up. Pigeons huddled on a children's climbing frame. Ahead of them, Nechells was an image from a black-and-white film: tower blocks, factory chimneys, expressways on concrete pillars. To their left, three gasholders marked the Windsor industrial estate. Two of them had metal walls, the third a skeleton of criss-crossed girders. The sunrise was a ribbon of dark fire behind the skyline; a flag waiting to be shaken out. Lisa and Matthew walked along in a dazed silence, holding hands. A dog barked furiously at them from behind a chain-link fence.

Within sight of the city centre, Matthew stopped. 'You'll have to go back,' he said. 'You've got school, haven't you?

So have I, but fuck that.' She linked her fingers behind his head and kissed him hard. Already she was wondering if today's papers would tell her what had happened. Halfway across the canal bridge to the bottom of Newhall Street, he turned and lifted a clenched fist. She returned the gesture. Then he was gone. Lisa wrapped her arms around herself and began to walk back. Daylight glittered from tower block windows and broken glass in bus shelters. The fire of dawn was turning pale. Lisa knew she couldn't go home yet. She stared into shop windows through heavy steel grids, gave the finger to a car driver who stopped for her, and lit a cigarette but couldn't taste it.

WAVE SCARS

Some people never really leave home; they just carry on where their parents left off. For other people, leaving home is what makes them who they are. Steven was the latter type. When he took me back to his home, it was to show me the things he'd had to leave behind in order for his life to start. It was very different from taking me back to the house where he was living in Birmingham. Obviously, there was the physical distance involved. And there were some factors which I still don't understand.

I'd known Steven for a year or so. He was one of a group of friends I used to see quite often, at the pub or at various people's parties. At twenty-three he was a few years younger than most of us, and had a disconcerting tendency to look younger still. Steven was so thin you wondered where the rest of him was. He always wore plain T-shirts or shapeless pullovers, which served to accentuate his fairly stunning looks. He had nervous blue eyes and a semi-quiff of dense black hair. One or two of our group had slept with him, but most of his relationships were with men of an older generation. Talking to Steven could be hard work. He spoke in a rapid, stumbling kind of way, with a strong Welsh accent. It was impossible to lip-read him, which you always try to do in a crowded pub. He amazed everybody when he got a job as a citizens' advisor.

But then, Steven had a way of surprising people. It surprised me how he and I drew closer together after Craig left me. I knew he was fond of Craig, and expected him to be quite distant with me. But instead, he used his knowledge of the breakup to help me talk through what had happened. It was partly that he wanted to understand. Craig and I had lived together happily for as long as he'd known us, until a newcomer had suddenly taken Craig away from me. The speed of it had shocked our friends. And Steven was nothing if not curious about people and their emotions. But also, he really did care; and some part of his diverse character felt sharply what it had been like for me. Maybe he too felt rejected by Craig; I don't know.

At this time, I'd moved into a studio flat not far from the house which Steven shared with two other men. The first time he came round to see me, I discovered that we liked a lot of the same books and the same music. I taped a k.d. lang album for him, and he introduced me to Dory Previn. That was the first time I'd heard that scary, desolate voice, cracking jokes on the edge of suicide. Steven also began to tell me about his life. A lot of it sounded pretty dreadful: a small town full of bullies and bigots; a claustrophobic family; a mother so transformed by mental illness that he hardly knew her. He'd come to Birmingham to study, and to live.

Recently, his parents had moved inland from Fishguard, breaking his most important link with the place. At one level, he was fiercely independent; at another, he seemed to be in need of a surrogate family – and in particular, a father. But he was already learning that familial instincts didn't sit well alongside other instincts and other needs.

The first time I saw Steven's room, I found it quite disconcerting. The walls were covered with photographs of semi-naked men, taken from calendars and magazines. Many of them were framed, some behind glass. I suspected that their role had changed: originally chosen to be looked at, they had become witnesses. But if Steven's love life was fuelled by adolescent fantasies, it was focused in an adult way. Anyone who tried to manipulate him very soon regretted it. He saw more and understood more than the people he dealt with. Many times, I heard him dissect another man's beliefs and perceptions with a sudden clarity that scared me. But he wasn't cruel, at least not often. He was simply judging people by his own standards. For him, being Steven wasn't a natural given: it was a craft, a vocation.

Don't get me wrong. There was nothing cold or scheming about him. But you knew everything he said and did reflected the way he had chosen to be. Part of him took pride in this. Another part ached with the lack of authority. Steven's personality was a labyrinth; but there was no beast at the centre, only a whorl like a smudged fingerprint where the tunnels had collapsed into each other. You could see that sometimes when he just fell into himself, sat in complete silence with his arms folded over his chest; when you asked him if he was okay, he'd either reply 'I'll be all right in a bit' or simply not answer.

We only slept together once. It took me weeks to find the courage to make a pass at Steven; and I didn't want him to think I was just on the rebound from Craig. Eventually I asked him in a nightclub, where he could walk away if he wanted to. I was as nervous as hell, though I could have chatted up complete strangers without fear. He paused before answering. Wavy lines of shadow flickered in the air around him. I must have been drunk to see that. 'I don't know, David,' he said at last. 'I'm sorry, I just don't know what to say... Best to leave it for now.' He gripped my arm, very gently. 'Are you all right? I'll stay here if you want.'

I shook my head. 'I'm fine, don't worry.' I could see in his face that the answer was not an unequivocal no. And although the way I felt was painful, there was a great sense of relief in having been able to try. All I wanted to do now was go home and sleep. Steven came round the next day to lend me a tape; he borrowed a Ramsey Campbell novel in exchange. We didn't talk about what had been said the night before, but he invited me round for dinner midweek.

Steven lived on an industrial estate somewhere between Kings Heath and Yardley Wood. That part of the city is at a higher altitude than the rest; so there's no skyline, which makes you feel exposed. The complete absence of trees didn't help. Outside his house, some children were kicking a football against the side of a van; the crashes echoed in the narrow street. I felt as though the concrete garages at the top of the road were on a cliff edge, poised to fall into nothingness.

We covered a lot of ground that evening, spurred on by a bottle of wine and the kind of still August atmosphere that makes you want to listen and talk. In a group, Steven would often become tense and take refuge in a kind of adolescent vivacity; but on his own, he was thoughtful and alert. I asked him what he felt for Craig, and he admitted that Craig meant a lot to him. No doubt the strength of Craig's personality had a lot to do with that. But it was also the fact that when he'd arrived on the scene, all bright-eyed and bushy-tailed, Craig was the only person who'd taken him seriously. Now it looked as though Craig and Michael, his new lover, would be going away to live together. Which of course was hard for me; but I hadn't realised until that moment how hard it would be for Steven too. In any case, Steven said, he didn't want to get too involved with anyone just now. And it always threw him when someone he was friendly with asked him out: 'I always think of... like, a beautiful summer night, and some perfect stranger who just comes up to me out of nowhere.' He laughed; it was a naive way of putting it, but I knew what he meant. It can be very hard to change the way you look at someone. I tried to reassure him that what he'd said in the nightclub hadn't offended me at all, and that he could trust me not to push my luck. I always think of seduction as a false concept; you shouldn't take what's not given.

He also told me about his mother's breakdown. It happened when he was twelve. He came home from school and half the family were there. His mother had been taken away in an ambulance; she'd tried to cut her wrists. Steven's aunt was still in the bathroom, scrubbing the blood from the floor. Steven went into his room, closed the curtains and wouldn't come out. 'I hoped she was dead. That's terrible, isn't it? But I couldn't understand how she could do such a thing. And I was closer to her than any of my sisters. She was

89

in hospital for a year and when she came out, she wasn't the same person. The drugs made her either dopey or violent. She's more stable now.'

I asked him if he knew what had caused it. 'I don't know,' he said. 'I think it was having too many children. Four of us, for God's sake. And she had to look after us, when she didn't even like children. To be honest, I don't think she liked being married either. But what choice did she have? That's why I had to get away.'

By now, it was nearing eleven. I said I'd catch the last bus in half an hour. Steven made some coffee, and we sat down together on the couch. I'm still not sure whether it was kindness or need that made him reach out for me. When we kissed, his head was almost perfectly still; I had to shape his mouth with my own. When I paused, not sure if he wanted to go on, Steven embraced me tightly and touched me in ways I couldn't mistake. He led me up to the bedroom in silence, and we made love more slowly and tenderly than I could have dreamed. There were points when he smiled for no immediate reason, and other points when he seemed about to cry. Every touch and movement and sound of that night seemed to echo in the back of my head. I remember one moment just before Steven came; he was lying on his back, and seemed to become entirely still, as if he were reduced to a single image. I glanced up at the wall and saw a pattern of blurred ridges in the air, like a crumpled piece of gauze. Then Steven cried out, and the illusion of stillness was gone. He slept very deeply in the night, only once turning over and twitching as though trying to shake something off. I never sleep well in a strange bed.

The next morning he told me, gently but decisively, that it wouldn't happen again. That didn't kill the friendship; if anything, we became closer. But at the time, I couldn't help wondering if I had disappointed him. Later I realised that his reasons went deeper than that. Perhaps I wasn't old enough; more probably, I wasn't a strong enough person for him. I rather suspect that, without ever letting me know, he decided I wasn't worth it. Even so, I didn't feel hurt. I could have told Steven that I loved him; but that would have made him feel threatened, and perhaps even insulted. He didn't want to be told that, unless by someone who had been with him for a long time and who intended to make the relationship permanent. Love wasn't a word that Steven used lightly.

———————

At the end of August that year, a burning summer turned into a strange, chilly autumn. Rain darkened the air for days on end. A number of my friends lost their jobs due to the recession. Nobody seemed to know quite how or why the government had been re-elected, but their economic promises were already as stale as yesterday's car exhaust. It seemed ironic that the people being made redundant now were the accountants, the salesmen, the designers. I remembered how 1989 had ended in a wave of global optimism, and wondered where it had all gone. There was a current of unease that affected everything. I saw couples splitting up, old friends losing touch, people hiding behind grudges. I began to cry a lot without really knowing why.

Steven went to earth, as he was inclined to do at difficult times. I saw him occasionally in the pub, and we met for lunch once or twice in town. He was more withdrawn than usual. Another love affair had ended badly for him, and he was beginning to doubt that two men could ever be happy together. I didn't realise what else was bothering him until later. In mid-October, he asked me if I'd like to go to Wales with him. He wanted to go back to Fishguard for the day. 'I don't want to travel alone,' he said. 'It's just that going home is such a ride.'

It was certainly a long and tiring journey by train – from Birmingham to Aberystwyth, then out along the coast via a succession of branch lines and small, iron-sheltered platforms. As the landscape took on depth and age, Steven seemed to come alive. He sat by the window, reaching out with his eyes. There were long stretches of hillside or quarry without any roads or buildings. When we reached the coastline, the sky had cleared; so that our first glimpse of the sea was of innumerable points of light, like a duvet covered in ground glass.

As its name suggests, Fishguard is a small town clustered around a harbour. We arrived late in the afternoon; the tide was out. Chained down in the muddy sand, the boats were ill-defined shapes under canvas hoods. Steven and I walked along the seafront until we found a bed-and-breakfast place. Steven hesitated before going in. 'Better ask for two rooms,' he said. I nodded. Even if we'd been lovers, it wouldn't have done to arouse suspicions in a place like that. As it turned out, the landlady offered us a room with two single beds. Steven spoke to her in Welsh, while I tried not to look as foreign as I felt. I still wasn't sure why he'd come here, since he'd said nothing about meeting any friends or relatives.

After a quick meal in a cafe where the only vegetarian item was some overcooked lasagne, Steven led me up onto the cliff path towards Dinas. A thin arm of land ended in broken fingernails. On the far side, a crescent of lights marked the coastline. Under the gathering clouds the sea was like a sheet of iron, hammered flat by the wind; the waves appeared not to be moving. On whitish areas of sand, I could just make out the pattern of thin scars left by the tide.

Steven was quiet; he'd been quiet all day. I didn't want to intrude on his memories. Every so often, as we walked back into the town, he'd point to some building or seafront construction and say 'That's new' or 'That's always been here'. We stopped at a pub, where a man with a guitar was encouraging the drinkers to sing 'Yesterday' and 'Let It Be'. Steven smiled at me over his glass. 'Weird isn't it,' he said. 'Places change and people change, but music... I don't know, are they being faithful or have they just got no imagination?' He sat in silence for a while, looking around the pub. Then he stood up, muttered 'Come on' to me and walked out. I followed him; he was standing in the street, looking frightened and angry. 'I don't belong here any more,' he said quietly. Instead of going straight back to the guest house, he led me up a narrow side-street to a viewpoint overlooking the sea. The harbour boats were tugging at invisible chains; further out, the sea looked and sounded like a gradually shifting mass of gravel. Steven frowned and looked out towards Dinas, where the promontory was faintly sleeved in mist.

'What are you looking for?' I asked.

He shook his head and stepped back. 'It's not here yet.' Although it was a Saturday night, the town was all but dead.

Occasional car headlights photographed the mist coming in from the seafront. Steven wrapped his arms across his quilted jacket, pulling at the sleeves. I didn't feel the cold as much; but even so, I felt as though I were standing on a block of stone with the sea all around.

Back in our room at the guest house, we sat up for a while talking. Steven described things from his childhood: learning to swim by diving off the harbour wall; the crowded house he grew up in; how the adults of his family discouraged him from making friends, so that he'd always be there for them. Several of his relatives were still here, he said, but he hadn't kept in touch with them. 'I see most of them at Christmas anyway. And I see my parents every few months, that's enough I suppose.' He went to the window and looked out. I asked him what he'd tried to see earlier. 'Nothing really,' he said. 'Tell you tomorrow.' Whatever it was, he seemed relieved that it wasn't there. We went to bed before midnight, too tired to go on talking. Darkness surged over me: a tide finding ridges and hollows in the sand.

It was still dark when I woke up. Steven was gripping my shoulder. 'David. David.' He was dressed; I wondered if that was because the room was so cold. 'It's out there,' he said. I got dressed without asking any questions. It was just after three o'clock. We felt our way down the stairs and out the front door in the dark. Mist was a series of blurred fingerprints behind the streetlamps. The sea was invisible, a whisper of movement. Steven walked one pace ahead of me. He was shivering. There was nobody else on the streets, so it felt like being outside the town. He led me up a stone staircase to the point where the roads disappeared, and there was only a narrow footpath along the cliff edge. It was difficult to keep walking, knowing that the impression of emptiness on one side was a sheer and unguarded drop. Steven took my hand. He seemed to know every step of the way.

After a while, he stopped and pointed down towards the sea. 'Look,' he said quietly. The mist was rising to expose patches of grey shimmering water. Sharp fragments of rock broke the surface, distorting it into a network of tiny ripples. The wind's teeth combed through the dark waves, bringing up highlights of spray. Then I could see what Steven was pointing at: a boat coming rapidly inland, between us and the promontory. It was like an elongated yacht, or a barge with a sail; the jib swung erratically as the boat tried to slow down. There were several people on board, and for an insane moment I could make out their terrified shiny faces.

A few yards ahead of us, a very steep flight of stone steps led down to the beach. Steven ran down ahead of me, gripping the rail for support. The boat was lurching closer, coming in to land. They had some kind of lamp on board, but they didn't appear to be navigating with its help. At the head of the beach, Steven lost his footing and fell over a rock. I helped him up; he was shaking, and seemed about to pass out. In spite of the cold, his face was drenched in sweat. We were still standing there when the boat hit something, rode up out of the water and then capsized. At first, I thought nobody had survived.

By the time Steven and I reached the water, a few dark figures were struggling towards us over the rocks. They appeared to be badly hurt. The nearest of them was covering his face with one arm. I pulled him up onto the sand before realising that his head was in some way joined to his forearm, so that there was no face to cover. Both his arms ended in smoothly healed stumps.

I turned back to the water, where Steven had caught hold of somebody and was trying to lift him. More of the survivors were emerging from the wreck. Some were holding onto each other. One of them collapsed as a wave struck him from behind; I caught his arms and helped him to stand up. A rock had gashed his shoulder, but there was no blood. His eyes and mouth appeared to be incapable of opening, so that his sealed face gave an impression of peace. He stepped past me onto the sand, and fell again. From behind him, a woman reached up with a child in her arms. I caught hold of the child; but her arms were joined to its body, her fingers spread across the child's shoulders like embryonic wings. A few yards away, Steven was carrying someone whose back was crusted with broken ribs. He looked at me, and I could see in his face the same question I was asking myself. *How could there be so many of them?*

But there was no question of what to do about the survivors when they were on the beach. They simply came apart. Their faces, if any, misted over with a pain so great it left them no identity. They became glass, snow, driftwood. They wrapped their damaged limbs around themselves, and bled their own substance into the sand. In less than an hour, the beach was empty. The only marks on the sand were the long curved ridges left by the outgoing tide. I looked out towards the rocks; but there was no sign of the boat. Then I turned and followed Steven up the stone steps to the cliff top. It was getting light; I could just see the outlines of trees and distant buildings inland.

We walked back along the cliff path in silence. When we reached the edge of the town, Steven paused. 'It's always like this,' he said. 'Every year. I need to come back. But it's always just the same.' His hair was matted with sweat, and he looked even thinner than before. I wanted to say *It's not your fault*, but I couldn't find the words. Back at the guest house, Steven lay down and went to sleep, still fully dressed. We had to be out of the room by ten o'clock, but I let him sleep for a couple of hours while I sat and tried to understand. Perhaps it was remarkable, I thought, that a grown man should be so imprisoned by his childhood. But it was just as remarkable that someone carrying such a weight of guilt and terror could still have so much to give. I knew he'd come with me, if I had a similar trip to make.

And it happens all the time. Boats go down, cars crash, houses burn; and damaged people spill out into the road. The only way to go on is to realise that it is always the same. You have to hold onto the few who mean enough to you to bring out the healer. And sometimes the healer is very difficult to find.

We left the guest house a few minutes after ten. Outside, it was still cold but the sun was shining. The tide had come in, and some children in cut-off jeans were diving off the breakwater. Steven looked at me. 'A Sunday morning and they're not in church! Maybe there's hope for them yet.' We walked slowly up through the still town to the train station. The platform was like a metal and glass shell; I imagined I could hear the sea echoing in it.

THE DEATH OF THE WITNESS

'Look at these.' Sarah blinked. There was nothing moving in the child's hand. Only some glass and stone fragments that trapped the sunlight. Ian dropped them onto the dull red sheet of paper. His shadow fell over them, closing their eyes.

'Where do you find all this?'

'By the railway. There's a rubbish tip. And things mixed in with the ground.' Ian held up a piece of greenish-blue stone, with the edge of a bubble outlined in it. 'Mum says this is *clinker*. Waste from a glass factory. Do they take the *colour* out of stone to make glass?' The window behind Ian's head framed the tops of buildings in the city centre, a mile away. The wire grid inside the glass divided the view into hundreds of tiny squares.

'I don't think so.' Sarah looked away from the intrusion of sunlight. The TV screen was too pale for the figures to be visible. Rachel's other child, Lorraine, was watching something. The children were off school this week; babysitting was one of the chores Sarah did to pay her sister back for giving her somewhere to stay. They were beautiful children, though they didn't make her feel motherly. She wasn't sure anything could.

By midday, Rachel was back from town. She was in a bad mood. 'Jim was in the post office. New jacket, leather. All he cares about is his image. That's all he's got. Told me he can't afford the maintenance payments. I said tell that to the court. I don't know, it's not worth the hassle. Five quid a week. What the fuck use is that?' She put her arms around Sarah. 'All right, our kid?' Sarah smiled. There was a sickly smell in the air: the paste Ian was using to stick his bits of glass onto the red paper. It reminded her of her own childhood. He'd made a kind of uneven circle with a space in the middle. From a distance it looked solid, as though the fragments had joined together. 'What's that?' Rachel said.

'I haven't finished.' He cut an oval shape around the brittle ring, then started to black in the centre with a felt pen. 'It's an eye,' he said at last. 'It's broken. The light's running out of it.'

Rachel tensed. 'It's not going on the wall. I don't know what's the matter with that kid. He'll end up in a mental home. I didn't mean that.'

'It's okay.' Sarah couldn't be bothered with emotions today – or memories, for that matter. 'Seen anything of Desmond?'

'Yeah, he was on the stairs this morning. Asked after you. I think he likes you. He's a bit weird, though. Sorry, I don't…' Rachel was genuinely angry with herself. 'Can't open my mouth. It's Jim's fault. I'm so angry, I'm forgetting how to behave. No, I said it's *not* going on the wall. Do as you're bloody told.' She pulled the picture down, loosening a few bits of gravel or glass that rattled on the linoleum.

Sarah started to pack away Rachel's shopping into the fridge and the cupboard. Eggs, cereal, tinned soup, bread. 'Thought I might go round to Desmond's this evening,' she said. 'Watch a few of his videos. It's only three floors down, hardly like going out.' She untwisted the neck of a plastic bag and tipped its contents into a clean bowl – liver for tonight's meal. She rinsed her hands thoughtfully. 'And you know what?' But Rachel had gone; Sarah was alone in the kitchen. The mosaic eye watched her from the floor, bloodshot and diverse.

Desmond's flat was much the same as all the others in Nash House; only the number of rooms varied. The wallpaper was older and dirtier than in Rachel's flat. But living alone gave him more space, the freedom of blank surfaces. Sarah stretched her arms and yawned. She'd felt tired all day – early summer was always strange. Hay fever put her senses on edge, made her imagine the wrong smells and colours.

'Mind if I put the light out?'

'No, go on.' They were watching a film. Desmond's collection of videos occupied half the wall behind them – from *Star Trek* to soft porn and a few horror films, mostly pirated. 'Shit, what is this?' The camera watched from a distance as the pieces of a glass roof rained down onto a young woman. One of the fragments split her skull. The face stared upward, bisected. For a few seconds, nothing moved except blood.

'Argento. Italian film. Really scary.' In the half-light, Desmond's face was simplified. He sat back down on the couch, next to Sarah. She wondered if he'd ask her to stay the night. Perhaps that was worrying him. In spite of the fiat and the video, Desmond didn't have a lot of confidence. He was nineteen, a year younger than Sarah. She wanted to talk to him, really, not watch videos with him. Bed might be a way of breaking the ice. It wasn't always, but at least they weren't drunk. She'd lost her virginity at a party, five years before, and her partner had simply turned away and gone to sleep. The morning after, he'd been as appealing as the washing-up.

Outside, it was slowly getting dark; a blurred mass of light hung in the air above the city centre. If Desmond had used the film to make Sarah cling to him, she wouldn't have played along. But he seemed drawn into the film, whereas she remained stuck to its outside. The camera was a cold eye, she thought; cold and distant, affected only by images. It seemed to know what she was thinking. It circled over scenes of butchery, keeping its distance. The terrified adolescent heroine stared at the misty hag-monster, willing it to be visible and real. It stuttered into focus, reaching. She stabbed it through the heart, and it dissolved into bloody threads. The screen was full of the creature's eye: red, burning. It didn't change.

When the film ended, Sarah reached across and took Desmond's hand. The tension in it disturbed her. 'I hated that,' she said suddenly. 'It was all bullshit. Pretty, innocent virgins and evil old crones. All the stuff about eyes and windows. What the fuck did it mean?'

He looked at her. 'Vision is power, isn't it? If you control the image, you control everything.'

'But control is not *vision*. Is it?'

'What do you mean?'

'Never mind.' Sarah folded her arms, like the girl in the film. She listened for the sound of doors slamming and footsteps in the corridor. 'It's not important. Look, Desmond—' Her hand stopped in the air, wrapped in layers of imaginary gesture. She couldn't make the first move. It was too soon, but it had to be now. 'Come here,' she said. They moved together and started to kiss. She could feel Desmond's teeth through his upper lip. Somewhere in the night, a window broke. Sarah thought of shattered glass and a bare grid of wire. It was the sense of confinement that was driving them together like this.

At fifteen, she'd had sex a lot of times with boys from the school in Witton. It had been sudden, emotionless, an act of rage that was only disappointing when you didn't come. Adult sex was supposed to be deeper – it was wrapped up in words like *affection* and *bonding*, if you believed the magazines. Relationships – like her parents, fighting bloodily in a cramped bedroom (she blacked out the image hastily); like Rachel and Jim, breaking up after seven years and two children. Since Highcroft, Sarah had been trying to get back to fifteen. Casual sex wasn't just a physical thing; sometimes, it was what your eyes and your heart wanted as well. Life is solitary confinement, she thought. Getting turned on and off.

The bed was tiny, and the sheets smelt a little – cheap cotton that pilled and creased, and absorbed everything. A white paper globe was swollen with light. Desmond crouched over her, gripping her shoulders. His face was pale and wired up with tension; his eyes moved under the eyelids, as though he was dreaming. Sarah wondered what he used to excite himself when he was alone. Magazines? Videos? What images did he fasten on? It seemed important. She closed her eyes as well, and tried to sink into a darkness where only the sense of touch could register. Within that locked room, the sensations magnified and echoed until she could disappear into them. 'I'm dead now,' she said out loud. 'I'm dead.' If Desmond heard her, he didn't show it.

Afterwards, he put all his clothes back on and made some coffee. He didn't seem to like being half-naked, Sarah thought. Was she meant to stay or go? Rachel wasn't expecting her back. But she doubted whether she and Desmond had anything to talk about. 'I reckon we're quite similar,' she said.

'How do you mean?'

'Alone. I don't mean we belong together. I mean we see things the same way. We like being left alone, not told what to feel.'

Desmond sat on the edge of the bed. 'What are those marks on your arm?' Sarah had to glance down to remind herself. The scars were still new to her, too strange to accept. And they weren't that obvious. He might have seen them earlier, close up.

'I tried to bite my wrists. Nearly a year ago. I was in Highcroft. You know. Didn't have access to anything sharp.' She looked at him. 'I've been out for eight months now. So. I don't like to tell people. They either back off or try to nurse me. But I reckon with you, it doesn't matter.' He didn't seem to take that either well or badly. Which was good, because she wasn't sure which way she'd meant it. She dressed, trying to distance herself from the situation.

'You can stay if you want,' Desmond said. 'It's not very safe outside.'

Sarah shook her head. 'Same building. Nobody can get into the block without a key. I don't sleep well in a bed with somebody.'

'I'll walk you up there, if you like.'

'Tell me something first. I answered your question, now you answer mine. When you're on your own – do you look at pictures? Pornography?'

'Yeah. I've got quite a collection.'

'Show me.' He looked confused, as if he wanted to ask *why*. 'I don't mind what it is. Show me something.'

'For real?' Sarah nodded. Desmond opened the wardrobe door and took out a box. There was a pile of magazines in it; he passed one to Sarah. She flicked through the pages, at first curious, then angry.

'This isn't sex. This is torture. This kind of stuff's illegal. And vicious.'

'Nobody gets hurt making these pictures. It's more playacting than anything. What are a few marks? There's no blood. You don't break the skin.'

'Would you do this to me if you could?'

Desmond smiled. 'No. I just keep the images in my mind. Like I said, if you control the image you control everything. It saves getting involved.'

'I'll bet it does.' Sarah was more disappointed than shocked. 'I must be going.'

'Okay.' There was no coat for her to put on. They walked together past the line of doors on the fourth floor, towards the staircase. To their left, a three-foot-high balcony protected them from a fall onto the paved courtyard. Beyond, the city streetlights were clustered like an insect's compound eye. 'Lift?'

'I'd rather climb the stairs.' She counted three flights. It was better like this – no struggle for words, no searching goodnight kisses. This was more practical.

'You know,' Desmond said, 'I was coming home once – about this time. It was dark. There were people screwing on the stairs. At least four of them, maybe more. I could hear them, but I couldn't see nothing except these lumpy shadows, pressed against the walls. It sort of frightened me... it was so strange. Unreal.'

Sarah folded her arms over her chest. When they got to the front door of Rachel's flat, she reached for her key. 'Thanks for coming up, Desmond. See you.' The door closed between them, and she felt as though she were already asleep. Moving gently so as not to wake Rachel or the children, she went to her room. Her little room with its barred window and whitewashed walls. And the TV set that allowed her to share the thoughts of the others in the block. She undressed in the dark and lay down, listening. If there'd been any sound – footsteps, doors slamming, people arguing or making love – she would have been able to sleep.

In the silence, you had to listen with your eyes. But the picture was broken up: a hundred facets, the windows in a tower block. *Ni nager sous les yeux horribles des pontons.* (Where had she read that?) The same window in every room – the TV screen. People were kept apart by the things they shared. Whispering to themselves in the dark, where the city's divided eye couldn't see them.

Why was it so warm here? She lay on the blanket, feeling her nerves tighten around her like a wire net. She was a prisoner. The house. The school. Work. The hospital. And now here. Why couldn't people see how confined they were? In Highcroft – the B ward, eighteen beds under constant watch – she'd found it hard to keep her mind separate from the others. Anything she did or imagined could be part of another patient. The only way to hold onto yourself was—

—to remember. But that was the problem. Years of blacking out her mind. Night after night, the shouting and banging. Shadow puppets. What did the sounds mean? The next day, she'd know. Bruises and scratches on Mummy and Daddy. One night she'd seen them punching each other on a bed covered with blood. Nothing that happened to her was as bad as that it had soaked up her pain, the colours in her head. Lying in her tiny room, watching the shadows thrown by passing cars – and the sunrise like a remote fire, a wash of blood. Nerves and blood vessels were your prison. The fireguard throwing its mesh on the wall. At least—

—they'd let her watch TV in Highcroft. And change the channel when she wanted. *If you control the image, you control everything.*

Except you don't. You're still on your own. In a hospital, in a tower block, looking through a window divided by wires.

The chain-link fence around the school. It was all about control. Being alone and being in control. Discipline. *There's no blood.* The bars were the view. The fireguard was the image of fire. It held back the blood. Otherwise—

—*if you don't follow the rules, you won't get better.* Lying in the still ward. Keep calm. Try to sleep. Get your dreaming over with. *Do you want to be alone forever?*

———

Around five in the morning, Sarah gave up trying to sleep. Thin sunlight reached through the bars across the window frame. She dressed and went out onto the balcony, which overlooked most of the estate. It was still chilly; the sun hadn't yet heated the dark pebble-dashed walls. There was a strange smell in the air, something like petrol or turpentine or white spirit. Sarah breathed in deeply. From the city centre, she could hear the vague hissing and scraping sounds of traffic. Nobody was visible in the courtyard, or anywhere on the grid of little roads that divided up the estate. When she looked down from the balcony, the side of the building tilted forward like a giant ship. With an effort, Sarah kept her feet and stepped back into the doorway. The sunlight flashed in her eyes like a camera; when she looked away, focusing on a place where she didn't normally look, she noticed the couple.

They were beyond the reinforced glass partition at the end of the walkway. They could have got there by climbing through the staircase window. Sarah walked up to the glass; they didn't seem to notice her. They were standing together, looking out into the tide of early morning light that glistened on their faces. A boy and a girl, no older than fourteen; both wearing T-shirts and ripped jeans. They were shivering. The boy was holding a Pyrex dish. Even from a distance, in the open air, Sarah could smell what they were smearing from it onto their hands, and onto each other's faces. Her vision blurred again, then came back into focus – as if she were watching two swimmers repeatedly break the surface of the water.

They were looking at her. Their eyes ate the sunlight. The girl reached up and peeled a scrap of pearl from the sky; she touched it onto the boy's face. They were painting each other with light. Sarah felt tears heating her eyes – prisms that broke and drained her, as though pain were only colours. The girl waved at her through the grid of wires in the glass. Still waving, she stepped to the edge of the parapet where there was no railing – and then crouched, tipping herself forward like a diver. Sarah didn't hear the sound the girl made when she hit the ground, seven floors below. She couldn't hear the traffic any more.

A few minutes later, the boy came out through the security door. He stumbled across the courtyard to the corner where the body lay, and knelt beside it for a while. Then he went back into the tower block, struggling with his key. An ambulance came silently a few minutes later. Two men put the girl's body onto a stretcher and covered it. Standing on the balcony, Sarah watched until it was over. The boy got into the back of the ambulance with the others. The engine started up, and the ambulance drove away. There was no siren. The iris-shaped smear of blood on the concrete paving grew darker as the sun climbed up the sky.

AN ANGRY VOICE

It was his father's idea. Which meant it was a game and serious at the same time. They were going to drive out past the edge of the city, up to the Clent Hills – if they could get that far. Mike, Helen's boyfriend, was coming too. Corin didn't really like him, but at least it would give his father someone else to talk to. They were taking guns, for shooting practice and protection. His father had insisted that Corin come with them. 'It'll show him how to be a survivor.' He'd rather have stayed at home with Helen, his sister, who was much better company. Often she reminded Corin of their mother. Which was perhaps why his father didn't like her any more. Of course, her not being his daughter didn't help.

The way out of town was difficult. Many roads were closed off, and others were damaged or blocked by rubble. You couldn't tell what was being destroyed and what was being rebuilt. Corin's father drove impatiently, braking at corners and swerving around obstacles. Mike sat with him in the front of the car, looking at the A–Z map and occasionally trying to outstare the skinheads in army uniforms who were standing at the roadblocks and checkpoints. Corin sat in the back, feeling uneasy. It was a few days before his thirteenth birthday. He wondered if his mother would send him a card. She'd left earlier in the summer, and they hadn't heard from her. Corin's father never mentioned her these days.

They were stopped at Warley Park; two soldiers searched the car while a third demanded their identification. The guns didn't worry the soldiers much; they were looking for explosives. Eventually, the car was let through. As they began to pick up speed, Corin's father shook his neck to release the tension. 'Little shits,' he muttered. Then something Corin didn't hear. 'Hardly better than the animals they're fighting. None of them got any idea, have they? Everything decent has just been fucked upon.' Out towards Blackheath, the road narrowed from two lanes to one; but he refused to slow down. Shops and factories gave way to muddy fields and patches of green hillside. Wire fences, supported by wooden or concrete pillars, flanked the road on either side. It felt as though they were being forced to take the city with them.

There was a sudden *crack*, and the car stopped. 'Jesus fuck,' Corin's father said quietly. Mike wound down the window, glanced out at the side of the ear, then closed the window again. Fragments of brick were scattered across the road. Corin's father tried to start the engine; it caught on the third attempt, and he steered uneasily through the rubble. Corin stared at the wire fence to their left. It was rusty, and torn in several places. Half a dozen or so men, all dressed in combat gear, were standing in the corner of the field. Some of them were holding pieces of brick or slate. Trapped against the fence, a few yards in front of them, there was a sheep. As Corin watched, one of the men took a few steps back, ran forward and threw. There was blood as well as brick-dust on the roadway. He wondered why the sheep hadn't moved; or if it was dead, why it was still standing. 'Maybe we should go back,' Mike said. 'Bodywork might be damaged. Can't get it repaired out here, can we?' Corin's father drove on in silence.

Higher up, the roads were almost deserted; the further away from buildings you were, the more peaceful it seemed. The bracken was turning dark, as if the wind were combing rust through it. Gorse bushes were snares of barbed wire. It was early September, and still warm in the daytime. As if reluctant to give up the protection of the car, Corin's father drove up a steep hillside in the shadow of overhanging trees, then along a ridge that twisted as it dipped and rose again like something alive. Where the road became a mud track broken up by clumps of pale grass, he braked suddenly and took a deep breath before saying, 'That's it.' The three of them got out of the car, Mike and Corin's father carrying guns, and walked up the footpath to the triangulation point: a short concrete pillar with a map engraved in steel. From here, you could see the grey outline of the city and the sunlight reflected in the upper windows of tower blocks.

A little way downhill there was a broken-down concrete shelter that had probably been built during the Second World War. Part of its roof was still in place; a young soldier was stretched out on it with a radio-control device in his hands. In front of him, a model aircraft wheeled and jerked above the steep slope, repeating its jagged drill over and over again. To Corin, the model looked and sounded like a much bigger aircraft circling a long way away. In the other direction, the slope was broken up by peaks and dips of land overgrown with bracken and rough grass. Trees shook dull flames in the wind, dropping ashes over the ground.

A narrow black scar on the hillside indicated the opening to a disused mine. There were several open shafts around here, connected underground but abandoned forty years ago. Corin had heard that gypsies lived in the mineshafts, hoarding food and other things stolen from the nearby towns. But the only people he could see were in a group down by the side of the road, working on a cluster of damaged and rusty cars. Their army uniforms were torn and stained with oil. They could be looters, or… what was the word for people who weren't soldiers but made up an army? *Militia*, that was it. But they looked just like the young men in the field.

At least his father and Mike had guns. The two of them were circling slowly, pacing up and down, looking for targets. A few swallows passed overhead, too small and high up to hit. After a few minutes, a magpie flapped down from a tree close by. Corin's father aimed at it and fired. Blood sprayed from its wing; it stalled in the air, forced itself back upwards and settled on a high branch. Mike's shot tumbled it into the bracken and dead leaves; he went to fetch it. Corin wondered what this was meant to prove. He remembered his father saying, 'Kill or be killed.' But where was the danger?

'Your turn, Corin.' He shook his head. Mike was walking slowly back towards them, holding a shapeless mass wrapped in its own black and white wings. Corin's father pushed the small gun into his hands. 'Do it.' They stared at each other for a moment. 'The way to hit something,' his father said, 'is to think of everything you hate. Everything that can hurt you. The gun's the only way you can reach it. Like using a telephone. Miss the connection, and you never get a chance to speak.' His voice was quiet and gentle. Corin gripped the handle of the gun, looked through the sights. The depth of the view fascinated him: a patchwork of brown and orange and red, like the hide of a strange animal.

'Behind you.' His father was pointing down over the slope, to where something was flying above trees. A large bird, black, clumsy; perhaps a crow. It circled and spread its wings, climbing an invisible wall. Corin stood absolutely still, taking aim. He was cold. The sun had clouded over, and he felt a shadow dissolving into the air around him like coffee grains in water. *Do it*. He tightened his shoulders against the recoil, and fired.

'Good shot.' That was Mike's voice. The crow had fallen into a dip in the hillside, overgrown with trees and bracken. It was further away than he'd thought. 'You have to go and fetch it, Corin.' He wasn't sure he could find it. Staring hard at the place where it had seemed to fall, he thought he could see a glimmer of metal: a wrecked car? He passed the gun to his father, who had just pulled two cans out of his rucksack. Trying to judge the right direction, Corin started off down the hillside. There was no footpath, and the way was repeatedly blocked by a combination of growth and litter. At least it gave him a chance to be alone.

The further down he went, the older and drier the trees seemed to get. The long summer had blackened them. Ferns and brambles half concealed the opening to a mineshaft, directly in his path. Corin felt as though he were looking for the centre of a maze. He could hear the sound of wind in something like caves or tunnels up ahead; but where? From behind him, he heard a gunshot and its echoes in the taut air. He looked up, but couldn't see anyone on the ridge. Dry leaves broke under his feet as he circled around the mineshaft and pushed through a dense cluster of trees.

Then he saw what had caught the light. It was a stack of empty oil drums, grey with rust and half overgrown by grass and bracken. They were spread in a semicircle to one side of a clearing made by fire. There were damp flakes of ash in the trees and the grass. Corin worked his way through to the blackened circle of ground. This close, the sound of the wind in the empty drums was like a chorus of blurred but separate voices. A man, wearing only a torn pair of jeans, was sitting on one of the drums. He was facing Corin. The dead crow was there on the ground between them, one wing outstretched. Corin stepped forward; the man didn't move. His skin was grey, hardened like tarmac by the sun. There were little cracks in the flesh of his neck and shoulders. Close up, Corin could see how strong the man's chest and arms were, and that he wasn't breathing. Only his eyes moved, remaining fixed on Corin.

The stranger was holding something in one hand. As Corin glanced down at it, he lifted the object and held it up near Corin's face. It was a rusty section of pipe, about a foot long, with one end flattened. There were rough holes along its length. Corin grasped the flute and tried to blow into it; the only sounds it made were harsh and broken, not music at all. He watched the still man take back the piece of metal and lift it to his own dry face. Deliberately, the man breathed in and then exhaled through the mouthpiece. A clear note rang in Corin's head; and with it, a brief scratching noise from the ground behind him.

Corin turned round. The only movement he could see was a cluster of ants just behind the dead bird, running around a smear of its blood. A few struggled or floated at the edge. The man played another sound; a black wing stiffened and jerked upward. Breathing faster, his chest straining, he blew a succession of brief notes. The bird twitched furiously, lifted both its wings and came at him through the air. Corin stepped aside, watching. The crow flew straight into the man's outstretched hands. He caught it and tore it to pieces, ripping its body on the edge of the oil drum with a silent, helpless rage. White tissue stuck to his fingernails like shreds of wallpaper. Then he pressed his mouth into the raw flesh and chewed for a few moments, before flinging the carcass away. Corin stared into his dark eyes. They were dry, filmed over with dust. He couldn't tell if their bitterness was real. The man reached up, and their hands met. The bird's blood was warm; but underneath it, the hand was as cold as a branch.

The sun had clouded over, reducing the view. Corin walked up the slope towards the car and the two hunters, empty-handed. Not far away, he could see the youths in army jackets, slowly dismantling a car that was soaked in rust. He felt powerless, safe only if he could hide. For a moment he tried to imagine being carried on the silent man's shoulders: the charge taking him straight through the gang of youths, breaking their formation, scattering them on the dark hillside.

When he rejoined the other two, they had already given up shooting at live targets. Instead, they had lined up half a dozen beer cans on the roof of the concrete shelter and were trying to pick them off from a distance. By now, his father was too drunk to hit anything. Corin tried a few times, but the stillness of the target removed his sense of purpose. Mike stared into the valley as if trying to remember the way home. Evening blurred the city, pulling it further away while bringing its lights closer. It would be dark up here soon. Corin thought of the times he'd been here in the past, with Helen and his parents. One day in summer, he'd been lying on his back and felt the ground opening beneath him, the clouds rushing over him like foam on a broken wave. Mike glanced at him and smiled. 'It's time we were getting back.'

Corin's father insisted on driving. As he waited for the engine to warm up, his anger suddenly caught fire. 'Pointless,' he said. His voice was loud in the small car. 'No sense in holding onto anything. There's no respect. What do we bring up children for? Families, work, the law. Nobody gives a fucking damn. It used to be safe.' He paused, looking straight ahead. 'We used to be all right.' He turned the key in the ignition, and the car jerked back to life. Sunlight prickled in the rear window. He drove impatiently, taking bends in the narrow road like someone flicking a cigarette. They were just reaching the crest of the last hill when he braked suddenly. 'Damn it. That wasn't here before.'

The car blocking the road in front of them looked as though it hadn't moved in a long time. There was nobody in it. Corin looked out the window: beyond a stony ridge, the hillside was matted with dead bracken and shrubs. There was a sharp *crack*, and the window turned white. A moment later a stone crashed through the windscreen, spraying

Mike and Corin's father with broken glass. It was as though a tidal wave had passed through the car and filled it with points of light. Through the gap, Corin could see two men in camouflage jackets. It was no camouflage here, in fact it made them obvious. There were more beside the car, forcing it to the edge of the road. Corin heard a brief, terrible cry, like an animal caught in a trap. Then the car tilted and began to roll downwards, bouncing on the rough slope. A door flew open and Corin fell into a clump of bracken, which seemed to burn against his chest and face and hands as the dirt rose like bitter smoke and the ground opened up.

A hand touched his forehead. He tried to blink away the shadows, but it didn't work. How late was it? His face was stiff with blood. The car was lying against a tree, further down the slope. It took him a long time to walk down there. The car was upside-down and looked different. Its paint was blackened, and the tyres were melted, and all the windows were broken. He couldn't see anything inside but darkness. The bracken around the car was flattened and scorched. Even from a distance, the heat scraped his face. His cheek was numb; when he touched it, blood soaked his hand. Why could he feel so little?

There was nobody else in sight. He needed to find help. Still dazed, he walked past the car and up the facing slope. Even though he didn't know where he was going, he knew the way there. Trees surrounded him like a maze. In the fading light, he could make out a grey stack of oil drums and a blackened clearing beyond it. The trees leaned inward, joined by shadows.

The man was crouching at the edge of the burnt area. The blood on his hands was dry. Ants were running over him. As

Corin approached him, the man held out an empty hand as though offering a gift. Corin began to sob helplessly, fighting for breath. He fell onto his knees; the dry earth stung his raw palms. The man watched him without breathing. Slowly, he reached out to grasp Corin's shoulders. The boy embraced him. His skin was cool and flaky, the pores blocked with dirt. There was no heartbeat in his chest.

After a few moments, Corin let go. The man picked up his rusty flute and started walking towards the car. With every few steps he sucked in a breath and exhaled it through the instrument, using his fingers to vary the notes. Corin followed him. Bracken and dead leaves crumbled under their feet; the ground below was firm and damp. From somewhere behind them, a dove was calling through the trees.

Slowly, a dark figure climbed out of the shattered car. Another followed it. They were almost unrecognisable; their flesh was stuck like dried mud on bones that hung at strange angles. They looked as though infants had made them. The man with the flute led them into the trees, still playing. They climbed the hillside one step at a time, each movement led by a note; as though the broken music had strings to pull them. Corin walked behind, feeling hardly more alive than the others. Brambles cut his legs, but he felt nothing. The mineshaft was swollen with darkness. There was a wooden ladder attached to its near side. One by one, the men climbed down out of sight. The music echoed, distorted by the tunnel. Corin stood for a few minutes, waiting; then he carried on to the roadway at the crest of the hill.

By the time he reached the final slope, where a stone staircase went down alongside the road, it was night. A cluster of orange lights was all that remained of the city. It seemed as distant as the three stars in Orion's belt. That night, and many nights afterwards, he wondered if his father was still walking through the tunnels that connected and overlapped like a labyrinth under the hills. But years later, he would think that the flute player's claiming of Corin's father and brother-in-law had no such purpose; that he'd done it for Corin's sake, to show him what it meant to be a survivor.

OTHER THAN THE FAIR

On Friday, Helen walked back from school in the gathering dark. Autumn was coming to an end; the trees along the road were mostly black frames. It was too cloudy to see the moon. She didn't like walking on her own in these conditions, but this afternoon she couldn't face the company of the other girls either. The house was dark when she let herself in. Immediately, before she had time to rouse herself with a cup of tea, the night overtook her. She went upstairs to her room and slept for an hour. The sound of Claire coming home woke her up. Still half dreaming, Helen stepped across her room to the dressing table and examined her reflection. The face she saw appeared still childish, though framed by long dark hair. She would be fourteen in a month's time.

Was this how Claire had looked a couple of years ago? Helen wondered as she changed her clothes and carefully applied some make-up. She and her elder sister no longer shared the same world that had kept them, as children, on almost equal terms. Claire had moved into a realm that was alternately threatening and glorious, overshadowed by boys, lit up by fashions. For months now she had been going out with Gary, who at seventeen was a year beyond her. Helen would have liked to be able to impress Gary. He was a lot more attractive than the rather irritating lads of her own age.

'You all right for this evening?' Claire asked her when she emerged. 'Don't look too bad, actually.' Helen smiled, flattered. 'Gary's calling at seven-thirty.' The three of them were going to the firework display on Midsummer Common. For Claire and Helen, who had moved in early in the new year, it would be the first time they'd seen it. Afterwards they might spend some time in the funfair. Helen had saved some money for fireworks; but the established family ritual of lighting fireworks in the back garden had been abandoned this year. Claire had suggested going to the display, probably just to get herself and Helen away from the house for the evening; she had promised that Gary would take care of them.

Helen's parents both arrived at roughly the same time. She could hear them arguing in the kitchen below; she put on a record to drown out their voices. Claire had to thump on her door to get her to come down for dinner. The atmosphere at the table was as difficult as ever. Whatever was the matter, it was clearly not to be discussed in front of the children. Helen resented that exclusion as much as she hated being expected to cope with the silences. She knew that Claire felt much the same way. Her father fixed his gaze somewhere between the two girls, and began a monologue about a firework display that he had been to as a young man in London. It had gone on for a full hour, he said. For the thousand onlookers, it had been like daybreak in a cathedral full of stained glass… During his description, Helen's mother turned to Claire and muttered: 'When's Gary coming for you both?'

'I see you hang on my every word,' said Helen's father sharply, and resumed. Helen's mother bit her lip. When he had finished speaking, she ignored him and spoke to Claire. Helen didn't catch much of what was being said; she'd withdrawn into herself, as she made a habit of doing. The record she had been playing upstairs replayed itself inwardly, while Gary mouthed the words to a black microphone, vitality concentrated in his face. Abruptly, Helen's father left the table. Her mother continued talking, saying something about school and Claire's job prospects next summer; but she fell into silence when the front door slammed. Claire and Helen looked at each other. It was nearly half past seven.

Their mother took out a little pocket mirror and began to comb her hair, which, like Helen's, was long and straight. Claire's was cut short and recently permed. 'Why don't you come with us to the fair?' Claire said.

'No, it's not worth it,' was the tired answer. 'They used to be something to look at. Even now, if you go to Brighton, say. There'll be nothing there tonight but slot machines and candy floss.' She got up and went upstairs. The girls put on their coats and waited for Gary. After a few minutes, their mother came back down, brightly made up. She went and sat down in the front room. Helen drifted in, confused at the way the evening seemed to be coming apart. For a moment, her mother's fixed and varnished face looked unfamiliar.

She was sitting by the bookcase, a pile of photograph albums beside her on the couch. One was open on her lap. It showed Helen's parents, maybe ten years ago, in the countryside. The wind blew her mother's hair backwards; she was laughing, in the photograph. 'I was beautiful then, wasn't I?' she asked clearly. Helen wondered whether she was meant to reply. The doorbell broke the silence.

Gary looked flushed, and apologised to Claire for being late. 'We'll have to hurry now.' He was wearing dark cords and a green army jacket. The soldier image, though it was put on, suited him. He was over six foot, but slightly built; he had blond curly hair and a rather gentle face. His eyes, which Helen had never seen close up, were blue; they always seemed to be amused at something. He led the two girls out into the cloudy night. They called goodbye, but heard no response. The three of them walked along in silence. The wind made the streets feel colder and emptier than they looked. Fireworks were occasionally audible from behind the houses.

A long road led up to Midsummer Common: over the river and along by a park, where a few tramps were sleeping on benches or the ground. Behind them, occasional lamps picked out the russet heads of trees flanking a great avenue. A children's playground, with swings and climbing-frames, hovered in dim light like an Ardizzone sketch. On the other side of the road, the Common was crowded with people. The bonfire was a solid mass of colours. Beyond the crowd, the fair was visible only as a mosaic of electric lights in continuous motion against the night. It had been there for a week, huddled in inactivity.

The three joined the crowd as the firework display began. Gary stood with his arm around Claire; Helen was just in front, behind an elderly couple in cheap raincoats. The empty, clouded sky beyond the bonfire was opened up with patterns of light. The fireworks went on for nearly half an hour, working up to a frenetic conclusion. Most of them were visible high overhead, tearing into the air in a steep arc and exploding at the turning point, releasing clusters of intensely coloured stars. The fading trails of sparks fell harmlessly into the audience. There was a burst of applause at the end. Helen felt as though she could still see the fireworks blooming in some part of her mind that she had not been aware of before. Claire and Gary were still quietly absorbed in the shared vision as they began to walk away. The three tried to readjust their eyes to the task of manoeuvring through the dense crowd. The bonfire was still in full strength; Helen felt its heat, a bright tension, as they passed it. The flames stretched upward like poppies in the neck of a glass vase.

The fair was rather a disappointment. Helen hadn't expected very much from a small travelling fair like this one; but it had seemed only to be the same few things repeated many times over. Most of the rides were tame and even childish: trains and roundabouts, or cars that followed narrow loops at head level. Hamburger stands alternated with shooting galleries, darts or skittles. Sawdust was scattered unevenly over the ground. The three wandered in a vaguely circular course, past rows of stalls so similar that they might not realise when they got back to where they had started.

The sisters watched Gary try a shooting gallery, loading metal pellets into an air rifle and taking aim at a row of little white figures. Two went down; the third shot missed. Gary looked disgusted. 'It's a waste of time,' he said. 'These things don't aim properly.' They passed on. The lights were all so bright that Helen's eyes had no chance to adjust to the dark; the gaps between the stalls were impenetrable, like holes in the world. Somewhere outside, people must still be passing by along the road or lighting sparklers in the bonfire. Helen watched the leather-jacketed boys in the amusement arcades. They looked different from the teenaged lads she saw in the shopping centre on Saturday afternoons. They were intense, directed by a sense of purpose. Their short hair was gelled into hard formations; the lights turned their faces into white masks, pulled taut over their cheekbones.

Claire and Gary decided to go on the Big Wheel, probably the highest vantage-point available in the fairground. Helen didn't like the idea of being suspended in mid-air for minutes when the wheel stopped. She tried another, smaller kind of wheel: a revolving disc where the passengers stood at the rim, facing inward. A horizontal metal bar locked into place in front of her. The wheel gathered speed, then tilted until it was vertical. Helen could see the circle of tense figures of which she was part; it was still, a line of reference while the rest of the world moved. She stared up into the massive clouds, then down onto the hard lights. It felt as though she was being gripped from behind and lifted within the wheel. She wanted to reach out and grasp the air in front of her, to hold onto something while the sky and the fair turned over each other. The shadows hiding the moon had merged into a giant figure.

The ride seemed to go on for a long time. By degrees, the downward view became familiar. Helen could see the bonfire to one side, and the road beyond it. But at the end of the fair, where she had assumed there to be only open field or parked caravans, something else was visible. She would have thought it was the after-image of the machines in the foreground, if it weren't so still. She could see bare silver-grey frames that reminded her of the children's playground; and little dark stalls, clustered like sheds in a back garden. The light there was thin and metallic, like moonlight, though there was no moon. Figures were moving between the frames and stalls; they too looked dwarfed in this picture. There were patches of dull flame scattered over the dim region, but they, like the movements of the reduced people, seemed to be held down or submerged, as though the air between Helen and that part of the field was filled with a heat-haze or with layers of translucent material. She closed her eyes and held on painfully to the metal bar, willing everything outside the revolving wheel to disappear. The music from below shuddered through her head. Guitars, a woman's voice.

When Helen got off she felt tiny and distorted, as though she had swallowed a fragment of the night sky. Her sense of balance was confused. Though the world felt quite stable she could not orient herself within it. The fairground no longer enclosed her. She imagined whatever was beyond it as a medium between herself and the vast night. When she saw Claire and Gary waiting, she felt an urgent need to communicate the strangeness that had got into her. But no words came through. The other two were quiet. Had they also seen something different? As she followed them, the gentle outlines of what she had seen gave way to the hard colours of the machines. Her eyes readjusted to the near range.

It had started to rain. In the light from an arcade, the falling drops looked heavier than they felt. Though mud, flecked with sawdust, filled every space not covered by boards, and dark pools spread over the more trodden areas, most of the crowd stayed. Gary bought three hamburgers at a van. Helen could not finish hers; she still felt dizzy, and the taste of rainwater mingled with grease repulsed her. The three took shelter by the side of a caravan, at a corner of the fairground near to the road. Opposite them, an evangelist was speaking to a drifting audience. Helen couldn't follow what he was saying. She wondered how late it was, and whether anyone would be in when she and Claire got back.

The preacher was pointing to a board covered with yellow stickers. As he pulled off each sticker, a word in capitals was revealed: HUMANITY, SIN, LOVE, FUTURE. 'People don't use God's words any more,' he said. 'They think they know better than God. It doesn't matter what God has to say. They ignore it.' His eyes scanned the audience and passers-by with impatience; each time he looked back to the board, it seemed to renew his strength. Helen was reminded of her mother and the photograph album. A little way beyond the preacher's corner, a rainbow placard advertised a fortune-teller's booth.

Gary and Claire started arguing about whether to cross the path. Perhaps they had seen something, then. Beyond a fringe of trees, some stalls were dimly visible. 'There's no point going on through this mud,' Claire said. 'It's all shut up there anyway. Why bother?'

'We saw some lights, didn't we? There might be a proper shooting gallery there,' replied Gary. 'It's not that bad to walk across, no worse than here. We can turn back easily if there's nothing.' He sounded determined; his eyes blinked at the rain, trying to make out what was on the other side. Without further argument, he stepped out between the trees.

Claire gestured to Helen, who stepped back. 'I'll catch you up,' she called, pointing to the fortune-teller's van. Claire shrugged and turned away hurriedly. Helen saw her pass into the web of rain at the edge of the light. She hoped they'd be able to find each other easily. To have kept her sister from joining Gary would only have created more problems; but momentarily, her confidence wavered. She pushed aside the fringe of beads at the entrance to the fortune-teller's booth.

The inside was dim and undecorated. A short woman of middle age was sitting behind a low table, on which a glass sphere was covered by a delicate-looking veil. She held out a hand. 'A pound, please.' Helen paid, though she could scarcely afford it. The woman took out a pack of cards and passed them to Helen, who wondered what she was supposed to do with them. Then the woman took the cards back and began to spread them over the table in a complex pattern. Helen did not recognise the designs; she supposed they were Tarot cards. The clairvoyant looked up at her briefly. Her eyes were dark, unblinking, and too large for her face.

'Do you want to know what you will become?' she asked. Helen nodded. 'Well, you will act. Perhaps for a living, perhaps not. But that is what you will be, an actress...' Helen had played minor roles in school plays, but she had done no other acting, unless one counted the endless solitary dramas conceived in the privacy of her thoughts. 'And you will be beautiful,' the fortune-teller went on. She looked intently at

Helen's face, neck, shoulders. 'Like your mother... You're worried about your mother, aren't you?' Helen nodded again. The woman paused; a look of doubt crossed her face, as if she didn't trust herself to speak. 'I can feel someone trying to escape. It's either you or your mother. Or both. But she won't succeed. The other side she's looking for is only a trap. She can't make up for lost time... But you're young enough, you can find a different way. To get out. Time is open for you.' She seemed to be speaking on impulse, bewildered by her own words. Abruptly she leant forward and Helen saw, with a shock, that her eyes weren't dark at all. Enclosed by circles of heavy mascara, they were a sharp blue. 'It'll be all right,' she murmured. 'You're too young to remember.' Her head fell back into half-lit stasis. 'Good luck.'

Leaving the booth, Helen felt badly confused. That hadn't been a proper reading; but then, what was a real one like? She had been cheated; but the clairvoyant, who could well have been drunk, wasn't really to blame. Helen had expected something else, that was all. The fragment of night she had swallowed was growing in her throat. She felt on unfamiliar terms with herself. It was still raining slowly; gusts of wind made the drizzle move in waves, like a curtain being shaken. Surprisingly, the bonfire was still active nearby; perhaps the wind had stirred it. A drift of ashes was blowing onto the machines, visible only in the narrow space of light between sky and ground.

Claire and Gary must be over on the far side of the bonfire, where they had decided the rest of the fair was. Among the confusion of sounds behind her, Helen thought she could pick out the song from the wheel. Something like *the night belongs to us*. She turned; the wheel was revolving in the middle distance like a giant record, surely out of hearing. The bonfire spread a vague light between the naked trees. There were more stalls ahead; Helen stumbled forward across a gravel path, hoping the other two hadn't gone home without her. The muddy grass fair, she thought, and laughed to herself.

Beyond the fire and the line of trees, it was very quiet and almost still. The night was reduced to a close sphere of clouds. The first stalls appeared rudimentary, lit only by a thin metallic glow that had no visible source. Helen had the feeling of looking for something already beyond recovery. On the sides of the nearest stalls, sheets of corrugated iron were painted with very elegant, complex human figures and faces. The paint must be luminous; the illusion of life and movement was as compelling as a plea, *Watch me*. And indeed, the starved and fragile look of the faces suggested that they needed to be looked at to keep going. Helen walked on to another stall that was marked with swirling designs like tattoos: roses, pierced hearts, dragons. The front of the stall was empty and unlit.

Between the rows of stalls, people were coming forward through the veils of rain. They looked lost and worn out; none of them was speaking. The stall opposite to Helen had a raised platform between an entrance and an exit, like a ghost train. The entry door on the left was open and unattended. A girl in a raincoat walked inside. It was Claire, on her own. Helen rushed after her. Inside, there was a long corridor like an aquarium, with glass cases on either side. Behind the panes stood a sequence of immobile human figures: infants or the very old, alternating. The tableaux looked like photographic negatives. Their subjects were either naked or wrapped in towels.

Helen caught her sister's arm. 'Where's Gary?' There was no reply. 'What's the matter?' When they were outside, Claire put her arm round Helen's shoulders, as if for support. But her face stayed remote, closed off. The first thing that Helen saw when they stepped through the exit door was the tattooed stall opposite; the stage at the front was now occupied by several people, who were busy making something with wire and bamboo or wicker frames. Helen watched, while Claire stood passively at her side. Soon the people had built a clumsy fence and were securing it in place with wire. Then they began to construct a roof extending back from it. They seemed to be trying to enclose themselves in some kind of cage.

As the two sisters passed on, the other fair they had walked into became more familiar through its repetition. The fireworks and electric lights had kept Helen's eyes from adjusting to the dark; but now, as her vision became more acute, new details revealed themselves in everything. It was rather like a marketplace at night, or a badly neglected model village. As well as the terraces of uniform huts, there were occasional machines: roundabouts and wheels, glowing with a faint pale energy, but not moving. Many of the stalls had a few people standing on them; they were either occupied in building their own makeshift prisons, or already frozen into passivity behind bars, staring outward. In front of one of the stalls, a fat woman with two large snakes draped round her shoulders stood and looked in at a row of trapped, rain-drenched men. A flash of lightning made all the metal surfaces tremble. As it faded, there was a crackle of rifle fire from ahead. Following the sound, Helen and Claire soon came to the shooting gallery. An excited group of stunted or deformed people were firing on a cage full of helpless figures. Claire stared for a long time – not at those shooting, but at their targets.

The lightning seemed to have brought the machines to life. The whole place was crowded now; though the passers-by walked not just through mud, but on sheets of water. Helen remembered the patches of deep flame she had seen from the wheel; they must have been submerged further, driven under the ground. It seemed as though the rain itself held light; falling, it made sharp near-vertical wires. Crossing these lines, between the stalls, were stretched horizontal barbed wires that looked ragged with shreds of torn cloth. Helen glimpsed a figure dancing close by. It was someone trapped in the machinery under the big wheel, jerking in pain as it spun round empty. There was no sound other than the creak and screech of metal, and the sharp cracks of air rifles. The fairground resembled a battlefield. Helen and Claire began running back the way they had come; the mud soon reduced them to a walking pace that was as slow as dreaming. Those areas of ground that were best passable were littered with torn newspaper.

The people in the stalls were also using crumpled sheets of newspaper to fill in the wood and wire frames that enclosed them. That made Helen think of the papier-mâché masks that she had made for Hallowe'en in primary school. She and Claire were near the line of trees when somebody stepped in between them, limping. It was Gary; he didn't try to speak. Helen could see a few long splinters of glass embedded in the back of his green jacket. The three followed the slope down to the fence adjoining the road. Gary stopped and slipped off the jacket. Its back was deeply scored; light showed through it. Underneath, his shirt was stained with blood. The two sisters helped him across the road. Helen glanced back, but could see nothing of where they had come from other than the four elements clustered together and mixed up. Air, water, fire, earth; from a distance, it might be something to look at.

As they crossed the road, Helen felt something pierce her hand from Gary's shoulder. When they paused she slipped the hand into her coat pocket and caught the sharp fragment on the lining, pulling it free. Gary was biting his lip; he looked very pale. Helen watched the rain dilute the red streaks from his shirt; they were slow to reappear. The wounds were not deep, then. 'He's in shock,' Claire said. 'But he's not badly hurt, I don't think.' A taxi appeared on the road and Claire waved it down.

When they reached the hospital, Gary was able to walk without help. Claire found the way to the casualty section, and spoke to a nurse there. Her control only faltered when she tried to explain what had happened. 'There must have been some kind of accident, I didn't see. It looks like a pane of glass shattered. People were slipping in the rain.' While Gary was being attended to, Claire and Helen sat in the waiting room. The nurse brought them cups of tea. Water dripped slowly from their clothes, evaporating in the warm air. The waiting room was crowded; many of the faces were anxious.

'There's been a lot of accidents tonight,' the nurse said. 'It's not surprising, what with the fireworks and all. And then this storm; the roads are chaos.' Claire had gone back into her shell. No muscle in her face would relax. Helen glanced up at the clock; they had been there for twenty minutes. The palm of her right hand was stinging. She remembered the glass splinter in her coat pocket, felt for it, and drew it out. Whatever she had expected it to tell her, it did not. It had not been just a pane of glass, though: the fragment was grey along one side and silver inside the other, reflecting. It was a narrow triangle, half an inch long. She reached out and dropped it into a waste bin, then sat back and shut her eyes.

It was nearly eleven o'clock. Helen hoped her parents wouldn't be home, wondering where she and Claire had got to. For once, it would be a relief if the house was still empty when they got back. The warmth and stillness of the waiting room was wrapped around her like a gauze, with only its faintly antiseptic odour to suggest that anything was wrong. Balanced as she was between sleep and waking, she was briefly able, as it were, to feel herself forget.

AND SOME ARE MISSING

The first time, it was someone I didn't know. Inevitably. I'd gone out to use the phone box, around eleven on a Tuesday night. This was a month after I'd moved into the flat in Moseley. I phoned Alan, but I don't remember what I said; I was very drunk. Coming back, I saw two men on the edge of the car park in front of the tower block I live in. It looked like a drunk was being mugged. There was one man on the ground: grey-haired, shabby, unconscious. And another man crouching over him: pale, red-mouthed, very tense. As I came closer, he seemed to be scratching at the drunk's face. His hand was like a freeze-dried spider. I could see the knuckles were red from effort. With his other hand, he was tugging at the man's jacket.

Too far gone to be scared, I walked towards them and shouted, 'What are you doing? The attacker looked up at me. His eyes were empty, like an official behind a glass screen. I clenched my fist. Fucking get off him. Go on... He smiled, as if he knew something I didn't. Then he got up and calmly stalked away into the darkness behind the garages. The man on the ground looked about fifty; from his clothes and stubble, he could have been a vagrant. There were deep cuts on his face, slowly filling up with mirrors of blood. He was sweating heavily.

I ran back to the phone and called an ambulance. Then I went back to the injured man and dabbed uselessly at his face with my sleeve. Now the shock was wearing off, I needed to go to sleep. I looked at my wristwatch; it was past midnight. There was no blood on my sleeve. I looked again at the drunk's face. It was pale with sweat and blurred by a greyish stubble. But there were no wounds. *Jesus*, I thought, *I've started to hallucinate. It's strictly Diet Coke from now on*. Leaving him for the ambulance, I struggled into the building. Living on the top floor meant I didn't have to keep count. The next thing I knew, my alarm clock was ringing. I didn't remember setting it, let alone going to bed.

The flat's okay, though it costs more to rent than a poorly furnished studio flat should. At least it's pretty secure. You'd need wings or a sledgehammer to get in. Before I paid the deposit, I asked if there was a phone point; the landlord showed me where it was. It was only when I'd moved in that I discovered the phone point hadn't been used in decades and was no longer viable. When I tried to contact the landlord, a snotty assistant told me it was hard luck, but they weren't responsible for telephones. I said that having been told there was a phone line, I had a right to assume it was viable. She said they hadn't told me it was. I thanked her for explaining, then hung up. My hands were shaking. Unless I was prepared to make the landlord a free gift of an installation costing a month's rent, I'd have no telephone until I moved.

A few nights after the incident in the car park, I woke up in the middle of the night. I'd been dreaming about Hereford, Alan's home town. We'd spent the last Christmas there with his family. I remembered the cathedral, the old houses, the hills out towards Fownhope that were so heavily wooded you seemed to be indoors. Suddenly I was crying. Then I felt something touch my face. Fingers. They seemed to be following the tears. One of them scratched my right eye. I lay very still, sweating with fear. The touching was gentle, but there was no kindness in it. A cold palm slid over my mouth. I pulled away, then lashed out in the darkness, cursing. Something moved at the side of the bed. I switched the light on, but the room was empty. There was nobody else in the flat. I was more scared than I'd been when I thought there was someone in the room with me. I'm a real coward when it comes to dentists and hospitals, but with people my temper takes over. A few years ago, I was walking home late at night when I was stopped by this massive bloke. He asked for directions to somewhere or other, then pushed me against the wall and tried to take my wallet. I pushed him hard, shouted Fuck off and ran; he didn't follow me. I sat on my bed, remembering this, staring at the walls of the flat. There was a picture of a town covered with snow at night, done in pastel blue and white on black paper; Alan had drawn that for me. There were Picasso and Van Gogh prints, stills from James Dean films, and a sketch of mine that showed an abandoned card table on a bridge over a canyon. I'd filled the flat with images that made me feel at home. But it didn't work.

Some evenings, my head was full of a violence I could only control by drinking myself unconscious. The new flat had been rented in a hurry, while I was staying with friends after the split. Alan was in love with another man: a bearded American, younger than me and more intelligent. Two years of living together, and now suddenly it was all gone. Hard to believe; but every day I had to rediscover it by waking up. Alan and I were still close; we met regularly for coffee or lunch in the city centre, to exchange news or just spend time together.

He wanted to go to America with Paul, and live there. Until that happened, I needed to hold onto whatever feelings for me still lived in him. Perhaps by refusing to let go of him completely, I was damaging both of us – as though the relationship were a kind of wound that we both carried, and which the contact between us kept reopening.

It was at one of those awkward meetings that he told me Sean was dead. I hadn't known him well – a familiar face in one or two pubs, always chatty, but genuinely friendly underneath the banter. He invented nicknames for people that were invariably perfect, and never malicious. One Sunday afternoon we met by chance at the Triangle cinema, and he gave me a lift home. He struck me then as rather subdued and thoughtful. We talked about people we both knew; Sean said he'd grown out of the scene, and wanted a more settled life.

And now – what, eighteen months later? – he'd killed himself. From what Alan said, he'd been suffering from mental illness and couldn't see himself recovering. I cried suddenly, briefly. Sean was only twenty-three. I wish I understood why so many people don't value themselves.

Why someone with vitality and humour and warmth should deliberately end his life. Perhaps its people like that who get hurt the most, and can't hide from it. Somehow they come to believe that they don't matter. And there's nobody to tell them they're wrong.

Everyone seemed to be in trouble that week. It was late summer; the days were hot and sticky, you had people wearing sunglasses and carrying umbrellas. That kind of weather makes everyone restless and uneasy. A couple that Alan and I had known for years split up unexpectedly, and had to sell their house in order to live apart. I started losing track of who was seeing whom, and which affairs were open and which were secret.

Jason, a good friend of mine, lost his job as the result of a pointless row. He was working for the council, answering phone calls from the public. A few of the senior management people had started complaining about the way he dressed. His clothes were colourful and stylish enough to have some of the grey people muttering about 'flamboyance'. Perhaps Jason was too stubborn for his own good. Or perhaps he felt that, after four years of successful work, he deserved more acceptance from his colleagues. Either way, he tried to shame the management into an apology by offering his resignation. They accepted it.

I didn't have problems like that at work, but sometimes the general level of unhappiness in the company was frightening. Our salaries had been frozen indefinitely, while mishandling of computer files had cost the company a fortune. The directors blamed the recession; but the recession didn't force them to be arrogant, inept and cynical. Nor, indeed, to be absent most of the time.

At the end of that week, I went out to the Nightingale. They'd redecorated it in black wood-chip wallpaper, with black leather seating. The effect was deadpan and oppressive. I brought someone back to the flat. He was a quiet, sensitive guy in his mid-thirties, with a strong Black Country accent. It was more for company than anything else. We were both quite drunk. He used amyl nitrite in bed, which only seemed to distance him. I tried it, but it just made me sweat. Probably I was too tired. When he climaxed his body was immobile, like a statue melting in the rain.

He was asleep when I woke up and saw a figure at the foot of the bed. It seemed hardly more than an outline, and it was somehow too jagged, stretched-looking, like some kind of satirical cartoon. It was just watching. Perhaps waiting for something to happen. That was when I first thought: *the antipeople*. I shifted closer to the sleeping man, touching his arm, his shoulder, his hair. But the cold feeling remained. In the morning we both felt a bit awkward, and didn't arrange to meet again.

A few days later, Alan drove round with some things I needed from the house. Because my new flat was so small, Id left a lot of possessions behind. I'd have to collect them soon, before Alan moved out. He hoped to be with Paul in New York by the end of the year. We circled around each other nervously, able to hug but not kiss. He'd already said that I could sleep with him again if I wanted to. Paul wouldn't mind – after all, he'd been seeing Paul for three months while I was still in the house. Moving out had reduced the stress, enabled me to get some kind of grip on things. But underneath, I still felt the same way.

It didn't happen until Alan was on the point of leaving.

I kissed him fiercely and started to unbutton his shirt. Lie down. Please. It took less than fifteen minutes, but it was as good as any sex I can remember. Afterwards, we lay there and rested, no longer touching – as always when we slept together. Then I saw the creature sitting over him. It was probing his face with its narrow fingers; the nails were broken. Then it bent further down and pressed its teeth against his arm, just above the wrist. The creature looked a bit like me, but not very much. I hope.

For a few seconds I wondered if I should just let it happen. It wasn't that I wanted to hurt Alan. But... why should I protect him, after what he'd put me through? Then I reached out, grabbed the pale things shoulder and pulled hard. My fingers sank into the stale flesh and hooked on the bone. The creature pawed at my arm, scratched it with one ragged finger. The skin turned white and hard. Then I was alone with Alan. He opened his eyes and reached for me.

After he'd gone I put a record on the stereo: Leonard Cohen singing about the vast, shattered love on the other side of despair. I poured myself a glass of gin and tried to think. Was human love enough to motivate life, to give everything a meaning? Or was it so debased that the only source of meaning was something above humanity? I didn't know. In fact, I didn't trust people who claimed that they knew. The scar on my arm was numb; it seemed to be frozen. About a week later, the strip of dead skin fell away.

From the window in my flat, I can see out beyond the garages, to where a semicircle of trees forms a natural skyline. There's a cedar, a few birches and a pine tree of some kind. It makes me think of forests, green places full of shadow and drifts of leaves; places where there are no people.

The last few weeks of that summer were close and humid. The newspapers were full of road accidents, murders, rapes. I can remember walking through the city centre and seeing the crowd of people suddenly blur and sway, as though they had all started to dance. Alan and I kept in touch; he was under increasing stress, not knowing whether Paul really wanted to be with him in the future. He was holding onto a job and a home while hoping that he'd be asked to leave them behind. He said he still missed me. We were uneasy with each other, not really knowing what to say or to hope for. For me, it wouldn't have been hard to forgive him. The most difficult thing would have been to trust him.

In spite of this uncertainty, the glare of madness was fading in my head. I was drinking less heavily, though that had never been the core of the trouble. Many people helped me, friends and strangers; and while nobody's help was crucial in itself, the total effect got me through. There's more humanity around than I've tended to think. It's not human nature that gives power to the vultures and maggots; it's only human culture. Dead things like money and authority.

The last time I saw one of the antipeople was in August. It was outside the Nightingale, between two and three a.m. on a Saturday night. I was drunk and on my own, wishing I had someone to share the taxi fare with or even pay it myself, but not have to go home alone. Opposite the Hippodrome, I saw a body crumpled against a wire fence. Somebody was kneeling over it. As I crossed the road, the figure reared up and gave me an unmistakeable look that meant, *Go away. This one's mine.* When I saw the face of the man on the ground, my skin turned cold. It was Jason, and he was bleeding from a deep cut above one eye. The creature's long fingers were pressed against the wound. I saw them turn red and stiffen like tiny pricks. They were hollow.

For a moment, I hesitated. It seemed impossible to change what was happening. Then I lurched towards them, almost falling, and grabbed at the thing's hair. It felt like a mesh of dry plastic threads. I was afraid the hair would pull out and leave me with no grip. But he tilted backwards and twisted around to face me, his arm stretching before the fingers came loose from Jason's face with a kind of tearing sound. The creatures own face was flat and expressionless, with eyes like holes in the ground. He fell against me, knocking me over; when I picked myself up, he'd gone.

Jason was lying very still, but he was breathing. One arm was pinned under his body. His face was like a copper mask, melting at the nose and forehead. I shook him gently; his eyes opened. 'David,' he said. 'My God. What time is it? I must... I got beaten up. Did you see them?'

I shook my head. You'll be all right. Take it easy. He stood up, then wavered and nearly fell. I caught hold of him, and we hugged each other for a few moments. He was wearing a crimson silk shirt which was dark with sweat. The cut in his forehead was like a jewel, and suddenly I thought of Douglas Fairbanks as Sinbad in a film I'd seen as a child. Still holding onto him, I steered Jason across the road and down the side street to the club entrance. They were about to close up, but I told them what had happened and one of their staff went to get some tissues and ice. They knew Jason. He sat down on the doorstep, quite calmly. There was hardly anyone about. The night was blue and warm.

When the wound was cleaned up, I could see a bruise forming around it. His nose and right cheek were puffy too, though the skin was even paler than usual. The ice seemed to lessen the pain. After a few minutes, we walked down to the taxi-hire firm. I told him we'd have to go to the hospital. 'Can't I just go home?' he said.

If you don't get that cut stitched up, it won't heal properly. He nodded slowly. We waited in silence, Jason holding a ball of clotted tissues like a rose stiff with colour. I bit my lip to stay awake. Eventually a taxi came.

The casualty department at the General Hospital was brightly lit and reassuringly blank. Several rows of plastic chairs marked out the waiting area. In front of Jason was a rather gaunt-looking man of thirty or so, who was explaining loudly to the nurse that he'd swallowed a penny and was now unable to shit. It had been three days, he said. I don't know why I swallowed it. It was just something I had to do. The nurse, with well-concealed impatience, suggested he try a curry. Nothing works, he said. The look of hopelessness in his face betrayed him. I could pencil in his background easily enough: he lived alone, was unemployed, an incipient schizophrenic or perhaps an outpatient at Highcroft. But no amount of psychiatric help could change the fact that he had no friends and no way of gaining affection from another human being. When the nurse dismissed him, he took a seat behind us and waited to be seen again.

After Jason had talked to the nurse, we went and sat in another waiting area, with red upholstered seats and a number of silent people, all with minor injuries. I thought about the antipeople. They seemed to be everywhere in this hospital, waiting just out of sight. Perhaps they hung around the little curtained rooms where patients were left alone. One thought kept recurring to me, something Alan had said once. *The opposite of love is indifference.*

Eventually, Jason's name was called and he followed a nurse out through the swing doors. I waited, still drunk but sober in whatever part of me reacted to what was happening. Half an hour later he came back, with fourteen stitches in his forehead. It was past four o'clock. Jason lived in Kidderminster with his parents; he'd had to move back there after losing his job. I took him back to my flat, where he slept like a child. In the morning, I woke up and lay there for a while, looking at him. If anything visited him in the night, I didn't see. He woke up around midday and left soon afterwards, thanking me repeatedly for my help. But somehow, I still felt responsible. Fourteen stitches are not enough.

THE FOGGY, FOGGY DEW

The grey van which stopped in front of the office carried no legend to correspond to the words O'BRIEN INDUSTRIAL SERVICES printed in grey on the locked office door. As the eight people who had been waiting on the pavement gathered by the van, a short man in a cheap blue suit emerged from its front. He ticked their names on a list. 'Right, can you get in the back?' They climbed awkwardly onto the wooden benches that flanked the body of the van, on opposite sides of a heap of canvas-covered boxes. The benches were dusty; someone coughed. The drizzle made a subdued insect-sound on the low roof. The van shuddered into activity; its interior was paler than the exterior, a discoloured white, and enough light connected the windscreen with the blurred pane in the back door for the passengers to see one another. Outside, the rain filled in the remaining pale spaces on the pavement.

The young man seated opposite Daniel shrugged his raincoat up above his head and pulled it forward, reversing the sleeves, until he was free of its shadow. The gloom diminished his face, sharpening its familiarity. But even when, a few minutes later, the other offered Daniel a cigarette and he saw the long, tapering fingers, he could not convince himself of the recognition. Too much of the past was at stake for him not to hesitate. But as the journey continued, Daniel suspected that the other was watching him in a similar manner. Ahead, the windscreen blinked repeatedly at the gauze of rain.

The van stopped in a car park somewhere to the north of Birmingham. It released them halfway up a slope; uphill, a line of factory buildings were being repaired or demolished.

In the crease of the valley, a slick road twisted like a ribbon of metal. There were no houses in sight; a new industrial estate was taking shape on the ground of an older one. Large open patches displayed only flattened mounds of brick and steel, flecked with clumps of purple-flowering weed; only rain and the eye lent them perpendicular structures. Where the road dissolved in mist, three black chimneys were stubbed out against the sky. One was broken in half, presenting a scalpel's profile. Inside the factory it was dry, which made the air seem colder. A corridor opened onto rooms housing nothing but unfinished monsters of scaffolding. Radios competed with machinery. The vast concrete-floored warehouse in which the eight workers found themselves was contrastingly still and quiet. Tiers of metal shelves, beginning some eight feet off the ground, formed dust-skinned ranks that were confusingly repetitive in the half-light. Daniel remembered how the public library had seemed to him as a child; being empty made these shelves even harder to distinguish.

Throughout the morning they swept the dust on the floor into ridges like Braille, then into mounds. It was so light and dry that the brooms raised little grey clouds whose outlines settled on the concrete. Apart from an occasional cough or sneeze, the only sound was the insect rustle of the brooms.

When they swept fine wet sand back over the same ground, the concrete began to reflect a thin light. The mounds were shovelled into wheelbarrows. The faint antiseptic smell of the cleaning sand drifted ambiguously over the original metallic odour. Someone in a white overall pushed a trolley along the dim aisle.

Daniel held a huge plastic mug of oversweetened tea between his grimy hands. He scrutinised the vague figure seated beside him by the wall. Had he seen it hunched over a desk? The figure shook with a violent sneeze; spilled tea played a bar on the floor. The man turned around. 'Have you got a light?' he asked, then stared. 'Hello, Danny.'

'Peter – I thought I recognised you.' Suddenly he could recall clearly the image that had suggested itself: the boy of fourteen, face calm, eyes unreachable as he leant over the piano keys. Six years ago Peter's father had died, and Peter and his mother had moved away to another district; they had lost touch after that. 'What a coincidence. How are you?'

Peter's reply disintegrated into a violent fit of sneezing.

He put his hand to his face; it came away discoloured with blood. 'Oh, Jesus.' He fumbled in his pockets. 'Have you got a handkerchief? Thanks.' He leaned back, pressing Daniel's handkerchief into his face. 'Sorry about this... just this fucking dust,' he said nasally.

That afternoon Daniel and Peter used a mobile scaffolding frame to clean the lower tier of shelves in each row, taking it in turns to push the frame along. From time to time they whipped the bars with their dusters, creating sudden negative-image flowers in the air. As each grey keyboard of metal followed the last, Daniel felt more distant from his own mechanical actions. He could not imagine stopping, though his hands flinched from contact with the uncomfortable metal surfaces. Hours later the two climbed down, wearing make-up of dust-bound sweat. They washed in a mobile toilet on the building site; as Daniel turned to the door, Peter was still scrubbing at his hands and staring angrily into a freckled mirror. 'Need hot water, for God's sake,' he muttered. When he returned to the warehouse several minutes later, his face and hands were marked with red scratches. The anonymous van, which returned to the car park at four o'clock, seemed exactly the same colour as the shelves. Vacillating between sleep and waking, Daniel hung the pale faces opposite him in a series of steel frames. Outside, nightfall was beginning to paint in the gaps between buildings.

'I think we might do it this time. There'd be enough dust in the atmosphere to shut out the sunlight for weeks; the world would just freeze over.' The Anvil's gloomy interior suddenly framed a snapshot of trees shattering like icicles onto a dead soil, weighted down by tides of mist. 'Be useless to stay underground. There won't be a blade of grass left on the surface. Won't even be air to breathe.' Daniel stared at the taut face across the table. His glass was chilly in his hands, dulled over with vapour. He shut his eyes and the picture intensified: snow crusted like mould over an endless plain, littered with bodies that glowed faintly in the dark. Abstract faces crumbled; they consisted of grey ashes, like papier-mâché masks. The men sitting by the wall had similar faces, patient and knowing. They looked up from their pints of Guinness as Peter continued: 'They say people fear the unknown, but if something is feared it becomes unknown.

'It's like a shadow, it destroys the ability to see what causes it. Eventually it pervades and disconnects everything. By the time the end comes you can't tell it apart from the past.

'Imagine, though, casting a horoscope and finding that absolutely nothing is going to happen.'

Daniel felt a gap widening between the words and their meaning. Was he drunk? Perhaps he couldn't hear all of what Peter was saying. The song on the jukebox seemed to go on forever without changing, dropping phrases like litter onto a neutral background. 'What about survival?' he tried.

'You used to say man would survive if he wanted to.'

'Well, perhaps. I don't know what survives. Is it humanity that wants to survive, or is it just flesh that doesn't want to turn into dirt?' He finished his pint. 'Christ, look at the time. My mother'll be worried.'

Daniel stood up; confusion filled his head like catarrh.

Only outside, where it was already dark, could he see clearly.

The clocks had been set back a few days ago. 'Come along, she'll be glad to see you.' The Anvil's door divided the jukebox from a barrage of noise. 'They're widening the road,' Peter explained. Wires that drooped plastic flags guided them through a maze of trenches and pits. A series of terraced houses were in the process of being demolished;

the glimpses of pale wallpaper, strips of green vinyl over splintered boards, a red metal staircase, were inexplicably embarrassing. Another house supported a growth of scaffolding, some of whose squares were filled in by tarpaulins. The next street was a row of little shops, mostly boarded up. The boards were patched with several layers of posters, some advertising events months past. Corrugated iron distorted a gigantic face. In one of the side-streets, so narrow that cars couldn't pass by one another, two old women in housecoats stood talking, bent nearly horizontal. They didn't move as the two men passed between them. In a gap between the houses a narrow canal gleamed through spiked railings. At the next house Peter stepped over a low wall, crossed a paved front yard and knocked loudly at the door; then he unlocked it and led Daniel inside. A wardrobe occupied the space between the inner door and the naked stairs, to the right of which a narrow hallway was painted orange by the lampshade. A chilly Picasso? Family man, woman, and child – stared towards the floor. From the front room there came a repeated sound of high-pitched clicking. 'Hello,' Peter called.

The sound halted.

Mrs Telford had aged considerably since Daniel had last met her. Loss of weight had sharpened the birdlike quality of her angular face, while her hair was thinner and paler as though it had died. Between her chair and the door, occupying half of the small room, was a black wooden handloom.

Her hands, which, like her son's, were long-fingered and slender, perched on the shuttles. Squares of completed cloth, their pattern lost in the dimness, hung from several of the wires. After the brief interruption, her hands slipped back into the involuntary routine of movement. The clicking of the shuttles synchronised with her words: 'So you're Danny Carr, I remember you.' As they talked, Peter shifted uneasily at the door. 'Peter told me about meeting you at this job, a strange coincidence, don't you agree?' She sniffed. 'Have you two been drinking?'

'Only a little,' said Peter. He moved clumsily around the room; the contrast with his mother's appearance made him seem heavier than before. Daniel watched the alternating shuttles, nearly hypnotised.

'You know how it is,' Mrs Telford said to Daniel, 'when they grow up you've got no authority any more. He doesn't listen, doesn't even hear me. And when he's been so ill—' Her eyes focused on a point somewhere in front of Daniel's face; he remembered that she was shortsighted.

'Just some kind of allergy,' Peter muttered to no one in particular. The abstraction that had been noticeable in the pub was taking possession of him. He drew away from his phantom image in the window and occupied himself with coughing quietly. 'Must have been the dust in that factory. It was only the first day.'

'Well, why not spend all of your money poisoning yourself?' Her hands increased in pace; she glanced at Daniel as if to say can't you see the joke? The patches of finished cloth shifted in position, like draughts on a board. 'Can you stay for dinner?'

'No, thank you. I've got to get home soon.' He was glad that was true: eating in strange company made him feel stupidly clumsy. But Peter had behaved as though he wanted to discuss something. He felt guilty about leaving now, while his friend was off balance.

'Why don't you show Danny your music room?' Mrs Telford said. Peter stepped forward, his face still in shadow. He reached out a hand as though to touch her bent shoulder, to make a link, but drew it back. 'You'll excuse me for not coming with you,' she continued to Daniel. 'I don't walk around much these days. My arthritis is getting worse.' For the first time, he noticed a pair of dull aluminium crutches leaning against the far wall, next to Peter.

The music room was upstairs, between the two bedrooms. It had clearly once been a child's bedroom, perhaps Peter's; the wallpaper, tacky with mingled dust and moisture, was the same sickly pink as the cotton curtains. Two grey metal bookcases stood to left and right, one erratically packed with books, the other bearing heaps of music scripts, some in box files, most in loose bundles. 'Most of the music was my father's,' Peter said. In the middle of the room stood the large piano that Daniel remembered from the front room of the Telfords' former house. Behind it, a dull brass Christ was dying on the wall, small as a pinned insect.

'You still play the piano?' he said. Memories jabbed him: Peter in music lessons at school, in the junior-school assembly hall, at home in the evening. The wooden mouth jerked open to reveal the pattern which he'd been reminded of several times lately, though he couldn't recall what by. Peter sat down on the stool and bent his head low over the keyboard, as though trying to read it. From downstairs Daniel could hear the insistent click of the loom; and from along the street, he heard the crunch and scrape of demolition.

Peter had been playing for what must have been half an hour when the lights went out; Daniel had listened in a kind of confused trance that was more submission than attention.

The player seemed to draw life out of the keys into his fingers, while his body and head remained as fixed as a sculpted embryo. One of the keys struck dully – the wire was slack – and he drew in breath abruptly whenever he touched it, or when he played an occasional wrong note. Every few minutes he either switched to another tune or waited for Daniel to suggest one. When the house suddenly went dark, he carried on playing; perhaps his eyes were closed. Daniel remembered that the local papers had carried warnings about the likely effect of coal shortages on Midlands power stations. He wondered whether there were any candles in the house. In the dark the piano, a cold and painful voice, limped on regardless; so, he realised suddenly, did the even click of the handloom downstairs. There was a quality both reassuring and slightly threatening in these sounds that kept him, silent, in his chair and listening. Gradually his friend's profile defined itself out of the grey.

He could see the piano and its hunched player with detailed clarity, though the rest of the room was blurred. No light came from the window. He could even distinguish the black from the white keys, and follow Peter's fingers on them. The tune was familiar, though he couldn't put a name to it. There must be a draught from somewhere, turning the room so cold; the walls were invisible, and he could imagine himself to be in a vast open tunnel. The figure in front of him was smaller and more sharply featured than before. There was less of a curve to the mouth, and the eyes were wider open. The thought let a few words loose from the tune: and the every, every time that I look into his eyes, he reminds me of the fair young maid… But he didn't want to look into the eyes. This was the face that Peter had worn about seven years ago. He hoped the illusion would dissolve before this image could turn towards him a face of terrible perfection. If only Peter would cough, falter or play a false note, it would set him free. But the notes plucked at him, drawing his eyes to the piano, where he could now see the strings and hammers forming the skeleton of a chessboard, one square vibrating at a time. Dust surged back and forth on the squares, almost making figures – the draught was coming from the piano, he realised. That was why its teeth were chattering. He suspected that if he looked downwards, he would be able to see the loom, the hands riding the shuttles, even the pattern on the finished squares. He tensed in his chair, captured by vertigo.

A mass of figures hovered, inside or beyond the piano.

They were houses in a street plan. As Peter used the loudness pedal for two harsh chords, the houses disintegrated. Some burned like newspaper, some were simply flattened. Others remained in place as charred shells, standing without roofs or windows. They could all have been card houses in the wind.

Human figures struggled in them like insects being tortured by children, until they had no limbs left to struggle with.

Even when the jagged ruins were softened by drifting grey snow, a few people wandered over the mounds, perhaps wondering where their homes were. One made a cross of sticks and left it stuck at an angle in the snow – was it snow or ashes? Whatever it was, it blew into people's faces and shrivelled them. Kings and knights turned to pawns and were captured. The curled bodies glowed faintly, like their own ghosts, until the grey covered them over. The piano's cold notes fell into the vacuum, while the loom continued to mark the time, a perpetual metronome. Daniel squeezed his eyes shut and pressed his hands over his ears. He wouldn't let this instrument draw the life out of him on its wires – but he could feel the response growing in him like unexpelled breath. Tears formed behind his eyelids. The despairing reached out for him with arms that stretched harder even as the flesh melted from them. Their faces were lost, but photographs of his family were stuck over the skulls. Before he could find his own among the faces, Daniel stood up and fumbled for the wall. Almost blind, he made his way by touch to the door. He searched for words. 'Goodbye,' said Peter, setting him free.

'Goodbye.' The movements that took him downstairs and outside felt arbitrary. The street was lightly smeared with mist; he felt warmer in the open air. There was a space in his thoughts where the edges itched like healing tissue. What seemed worst to him was how the feeling from within himself had suddenly closed off. It had been too easy to walk away, there should have been more sense of decision. On the horizon, streetlamps were reduced to slanted eyes. The road-menders had packed up for the night; their trenches by the pavement appeared bottomless. It was some time before he happened to find the bus stop. Every vehicle that passed was transformed into anonymous grey. As Daniel finally stepped onto the bus it occurred to him that he'd forgotten to say goodbye to Mrs Telford. He would apologise when he saw Peter at work on Monday.

There was no work until the following Thursday, however, and the group Daniel found himself in was mostly different from that of the first week. Peter was not among them. 'I've no idea,' the foreman said when Daniel asked, 'probably he found another job.' Another van, almost indistinguishable from the first, ferried them to a series of small factories where they packed boxes with sawdust, polished machinery until it shone like bone. Daniel eventually became fascinated by the pattern the company's activity was forming in the city. He was reminded of a novel he'd once read which suggested a hidden meaning in the architecture of San Francisco; the idea had so many applications that at times only a growing insecurity could pull him out of speculation. In a similar way, he began to find that he could listen to the radio for hours while he tried to link the underlying threads in the music. He played his records until he could hold every note and space in his mind, where he replayed them at different speeds. The language of musical notation surely wasn't adequate. It might conceal another language, he realised, that contained messages. Perhaps a way in which ghosts could communicate. A dead language. Daniel knew that these patterns were illusory, but it didn't matter. At least they responded to minds, which no object could. Weeks went past while he placed abstractions between himself and Peter; and nothing changed, except that the day shrank like a window between the curtains of night, and the patterns of leaves on the sky and the pavement became simpler.

One night he dreamed an idea and lay awake, thinking it out, while the moon appeared and vanished. If he cast a grid over a map of the city and used it as a chessboard (playing against himself, as he was used to doing), the movements of the winning pieces would tell him where the company's influence was directed. The losing king's position would tell him where Peter's house was; he'd forgotten the address, and their name wasn't in the phone book. He was shivering in a dressing-gown, searching through his shelves for a non-existent town plan, when the pattern allowed him to admit that he could probably find Peter's house by memory. He hurried back to bed and pressed his eyes into the pillow before they could project the previous night's dream. He'd been lying in the middle of a small bedroom, with pink curtains and a dull crucifix on the wall. A man had stepped towards him in the half-light; his face was invisible, but his outstretched hands were dark with soot. Just before touching him the hands had drawn back to peel off thin grey gloves, which he'd hung up like paper bags on the crucifix. But when they had fluttered back to him, the hands were still grey.

When he got off the bus, the fixed cloudless brightness of the November day made the facades of houses resemble postcards. Gaps made by demolition punctuated the series.

Daniel tried to ignore the sequence of missing buildings; the pattern might lead him astray. If this was the right way, they must have filled in some of the trenches and dug new ones.

He was becoming certain that he'd lost his way when a Watneys pub held up the black weight of its name on a sign: The Anvil. On a bench outside, two men sat asleep, cocooned in layers of frayed clothing. He could recognise some of the posters on the boards – somebody had scratched out the middle of the word WORKERS to expose a pop star's face – but the dissected house whose red staircase he'd seen was now a patch of rubble-strewn ground where weeds were already growing. On the off-white side wall of the next house, graffiti were interlaced so densely at eye level that you could read anything into the scribbling. Surely this was the road, where a young boy in cut-off jeans was running across to bowl a tennis ball into the passageway between two houses. Dodging the airborne stroke that followed, he walked down and examined each house for signs of familiarity. Unexpectedly, he found himself looking through a line of railings; below, a drowned-looking black barge was adrift on the canal, its curtains drawn. Neither the boat nor the litter of leaves and twigs on the surface appeared to be moving. It was the next house, he remembered; but it had a ragged privet hedge instead of a wall, enclosing rose bushes stripped down to thorns. He must be in the wrong street, he realised, but recognised the house opposite as he turned. One of its upper windows wore a board like an eye patch now.

There was no answer to his knock, but the flaking door creaked open at the pressure. The inner door was ajar; he pushed through it. 'Hello? Mrs Telford?' Then he coughed at the sharp dust which the draught loosed from the carpet.

Damp painted a forest in the hall. Dust filled in the angles of the stairs. Obviously this house, whatever it was, had not been lived in for years.

From the unlit front room there came a regular clicking sound.

'Hello? Come in.' It was her voice. The carpet felt puffy underfoot. In the front room he could hear water dripping onto the ceiling. The window where Peter had flinched from his reflection had been smashed as well, but not boarded.

The draught took the door from his hand and slammed it.

'Oh, Danny. It's you.' Mrs Telford's bright eyes didn't focus at all. She was running the shuttles back and forth on the loom as efficiently as ever, though the wood seemed darker and warped out of true. There were no threads attached to the shuttles.

'Is Peter here?' Daniel said, and sneezed painfully, 'I've finished the cloth, look!' She pointed to a thick roll on the tea-table. Daniel repeated his question.

'He's upstairs. In the music room.' Daniel made his way cautiously up the uneven stairs, holding onto the banister until it suddenly lurched away from the wall. The door to the music room was open. He looked in at the figure hunched over the piano. Peter's hands ran over the keys, but no sound came. Daniel shivered; was he deaf? Sweat tickled his back like a cold wire. There was a strong antiseptic smell in the room. He sneezed again, and heard it.

'Peter. It's Danny, what are you doing?' The silent performance continued. Daniel crossed the floor towards the helpless Christ, then turned to the piano. Peter's eyes were closed; he did not appear to be breathing. Tiny clouds of dust appeared from between the keys as he played. Now that he was close, Daniel could make out an almost entirely muffled thud from within the piano at each note. He realised that it was choked up with dust. In the middle of a tune, Peter stopped and opened his eyes.

'Peter. What's wrong?' The player looked at his hands.

They were scrubbed pink and recently marked with scratches. Dust was beginning to smear the fingertips. Some black material was lodged under the nails. Slowly, he began to rub his hands, like a Lady Macbeth in a silent film, and then to rip at the skin with his nails. Blood ran down onto the piano keys. Daniel's face flushed, but he couldn't cry, he was not capable of it. When his hands were red-gloved, Peter reached down under the stool and lifted a large bottle and a wad of cotton wool. He dabbed antiseptic solution from the bottle onto his hands, wiped away the diluted stain, and swabbed the skin clean with fresh solution. His expression had still not changed (indeed, he wore no expression at all) as he put away the bottle and the cotton wool and, closing his eyes, commenced to play what looked like the same tune as before.

Descending the stairs less carefully than he had climbed them, Daniel stood for a while in the hall, then went back into the front room. Mrs Telford looked up at him and smiled. Her hands still shifted the vacant shuttles. 'Look at the tapestry, go on. It's finished.' He picked up the bundle of cloth and unrolled it. The material was soft and light, pleasant to the touch. He held it up to the light: the pattern was composed of innumerable tiny black and white squares.

'Stand back from it,' she said. 'Then you'll see what it is.'

Daniel spread it on the floor and looked down. He stared for some time. Then he looked straight up at Mrs Telford.

'I can't see anything in it.' He rolled up the cloth tightly and set it back on the table.

'Then you'll be all right,' she said. 'It can't hurt you.' She watched the non-existent threads on her loom. Her hands slid back and forth, regular as a pendulum. A few minutes later, she said: 'That's all, you've nothing to do here. Goodbye.'

Daniel was outside and anaesthetised by the cold, sharp winter air before he realised that, for the second time, he had forgotten to say goodbye to Mrs Telford. He continued to walk towards the bus stop, still wondering quite what had

166

changed in him. But it was too difficult to know. He found himself wishing it would rain, though the sound would be entirely drowned out by the rush-hour traffic.

WAITING FOR A TRAIN

Everything was still and clear, as though the day were holding its breath. Frost took the colour out of the trees. Jason cupped his hands and blew into them as the sound of the approaching train echoed from beyond the red bridge. The platform was crowded, but nobody moved towards the line as the dark head of the InterCity train emerged from the tunnel. No doubt they were waiting for the second-class carriages. Jason was so relieved at not having to queue to get onto the train when it eventually stopped that he didn't immediately realise he was the only one.

The carriage was half full of dazed-looking commuters, their sleep still ingrained in their faces like stubble. Most of them wore scarves and gloves. On the platform a crowd of people were still waiting, huddled in postures that suggested a lack of expectation. Some of them were reading books or newspapers; others stared through the train with eyes it was impossible to meet. Behind them, two porters were trying to wheel a huge box down a stone ramp that was badly in need of repair.

The carriage window framed a series of landscapes. A gravel yard was filled with the rusting shells of cars, piled ten or twenty deep. The Dunlop tyre factory occupied a valley, surrounded by a pale forest of electricity pylons. Further out, the bare fields were a crumpled quilt with its stitches broken; three cooling towers breathed shadow into the white sky. The only things moving were flocks of birds in the distance, their arrowhead formations tilting on an invisible mirror. Jason tried to lose himself in the view, pretending the frames moved in time rather than in space. There was a tightness in his chest which he identified as hunger. He couldn't remember when he'd last eaten.

Wasn't the buffet carriage nearer the front of the train? He stood up and walked through a series of long half-empty carriages, where the passengers sat immobile (in silence or with headphones), their eyes shut. The buffet compartment had no seats of its own; all the food was tightly sealed in plastic, to be taken away. Jason bought some coffee and a sandwich, then sat down in the nearest seat. He had no luggage to worry about. All the people in this carriage appeared to be eating; none of them were sat together or talking. His sandwich turned out to be rancid, part dry and part soggy, with a pale spot at one corner. The coffee was barely drinkable; there was a greyish sediment at the bottom of the cup that made him wish he'd left it alone. This had to be worth a complaint. Between Jason's seat and the buffet carriage, a man with shiny-gelled hair was quietly eating a large beefburger which smelt of rot and tomato ketchup.

Jason could see white things moving through the meat, like loose teeth that had gone soft. He got up quickly and walked in the opposite direction.

Between carriages, he pushed down the window and let the frozen airstream scour his face. His eyes watered, blurring the view. There were no factories out, here; only fields of white and gold stubble and bare trees like stained-glass windows without the glass. Beyond the ragged line of hedges, Jason thought he could glimpse the edge of a lake. Slowly, his nausea faded until he felt calm and sure of himself. The landscape was too real for him to pass through it. He twisted the door handle; it flew out of his hand as the door slammed against the carriage wall. The wind surrounded him like a bandage which slowly came unravelled as he stepped out towards the field. Before his feet could touch the grass, the railway tracks rushed up to brand him.

It was night, somewhere close to Wolverhampton and heading north. The train was almost empty. Jason had been playing cards with himself for hours, and wishing he had some music to listen to. A red gleam in the distance made him look up. There was a fire somewhere, outlining the roof-tops in between; it seemed close because it was so bright. Around it, white streetlamps climbed into the sky. The train passed a factory with strange metallic pipes draped around its walls; an automatic light patrolled the vacant shop floor. Pieces of glass twinkled from a row of giant scrapheaps. Then he was looking down at the back yards of terraced houses, reaching almost to the railway. He could see the concrete paving, the washing lines, the curtained windows that framed inaccessible lives. Then more scrapheaps,

171

towers, structures of aluminium and glass. And then the tunnel, vast and familiar as an empty bed.

The dark made him feel exposed. Was nobody else awake? Towards the back of the carriage, some people were slumped in their seats; an elderly couple were sleeping with their heads together, like a double exposure. All the faces were like curtained windows. Stepping quietly, Jason passed through the automatic doors to the next carriage. Three women were sitting at a table in semi-darkness. Their hands were moving; when he got closer, Jason saw that they were passing a single photograph around between themselves, always the same way. It was too dark to see what image they were sharing. He looked around: there was nobody else in sight.

Between that carriage and the next, someone was standing by the window and looking out. Jason could see the side of her face, and a shadowy reflection superimposed on the outlines of hedges and trees. She was young, about Jason's age, and had short black hair and a pale face. As he stepped past her, the girl turned. 'Hello.' Jason stared at her. Nobody had spoken to him on this train. She looked tired and edgy; perhaps she too was having trouble sleeping. 'Who are you?' she said.

'I'm Jason.' It was draughty in the space between carriages. The floor jerked sideways, making him feel unstable. 'Who are you?' She reminded him of Adele, his girlfriend at technical college. Behind her head, a few station lights were moving very slowly. The sound of the train dried out to a waiting vibration.

'Carol,' she said. 'Look. I want you to see something.' She turned back to the window and pointed with her eyes.

Jason could see people standing on the station platform, and others sitting at the back. Nobody moved towards the train. In the thin light from behind them, their clothes and faces had no colour. They were very still, as though they had been waiting a long time. Carol turned round. 'Why don't they do something?' she said. 'Every station. I half want to get out and join them.' She looked at him. 'Stay here a bit.' The lights began to slide away to the right; the train was breathing again. Above the blackened rooftops, grey clouds stood out against the night. Jason stood next to Carol, trying to share what she saw. Occasional lights revealed a flat wasteland where clumps of grass were mixed with various debris: rubber tyres, scrap metal, burnt plastic, coils of wire. Carol gripped his hand. Her fingers were cold, but no worse than his.

Her mouth was warm, though. When they started kissing, Jason felt something shift inside him, like a hand of loneliness reaching up through his lungs. Carol's need matched his so exactly that she could have been his double. 'Stay with me,' she repeated, 'don't go away.' He could hear the uneven beating of her heart. They lay down together. The difficulty of making love in a confined space, the slight discomfort and confusion, gave him an unexpected sense of reality. The train's jolts and vibrations passed through them both, as though they were part of it and not just its passengers. The journey was theirs.

After the climax, they slipped apart. Jason felt numb and helpless, as though a current had been switched off. Carol recovered herself more quickly. She straightened her clothes and glanced at the window. 'They're still there,' she said. 'It's cold.' She wrapped her arms around herself and gave him a kind of frightened smile. 'Stay with me. I want you to see something.' She took his hand and led him through the door to the toilet: a tiny room with a washbasin, a hand-towel and a condom machine.

'What is it? What's up?' There was nothing to see in here. There wasn't even a window. Carol looked even paler than before. She fumbled in the pockets of her denim jacket and brought out a little plastic box. It was full of new razor blades. Before Jason could say anything, she cut herself across the inside of her left wrist. A gash opened and, seconds later, began to bleed. She knelt down and held her wrist over the toilet bowl. Blood ran through the fingers. Jason knelt beside her and stroked her hair; he didn't know what else to do.

After a minute or so, Carol flushed the toilet. 'It goes over the tracks,' she said. 'The whole fucking line. It's my signature. Backwards and forwards.' She was crying quietly. The tears ran from her face into the rusty water. Jason tried to pull her away, but her muscles were rigid. Someone else would have to find her. As he closed the door behind him, he heard Carol flushing the toilet again. What did it mean, he wondered, when the acts you lived by were only gestures? But he didn't have time to think about it. The train had stopped; in the window, a city's distant lights were sprawled like a constellation. There must be some problem with the line ahead. Jason twisted the door handle and carefully pushed the door half open. One sideways step, and he was able to climb onto the metal struts between the carriages. From there, it was easy to pull himself up onto the carriage roof. He crouched there, with his hands and feet lodged in a metal grid. The cold made his fingers ache. Soon the train started up again; Jason tensed himself against the wind. Not far ahead, he could see the mouth of a tunnel where the railway passed under a road. He saw half the train disappear, its roar muffled by the sleeve of darkness; and when he was near enough to see a lorry on the road above the train, he put his hands over his face and stood up.

There was a brick-red glow on the skyline, the effect, of either distant rainfall or fire. Jason could see pieces of the sky in the windows of derelict buildings. Quite a few people got on the train at Coventry; but most of them stayed on the platform. This time, he saw them clearly. He saw how many of them were crowded onto each seat, behind each face. Waiting for the train. Whatever it was that came to take them to another place or to reunite them with their families, it wasn't the train. It was just a vehicle, a machine on rails; not the train. Around him, people were storing luggage and looking for empty seats. Three of the newcomers sat around a table just across the aisle from Jason. They were his parents and his younger sister. He turned to face them; they didn't react.

Half an hour later, they were still ignoring him. Only his sister, Catherine, had thrown him a few secretive glances.

Twice his father muttered something to his mother, and she nodded. They both looked tired and uneasy. How much longer could they keep this up? Suddenly, all three of them stood up and headed for the far end of the carriage. Jason had a clear view of the window where they had been: a sign read STAFFORD. He'd have to follow them out. But other people were blocking his way; by the time he'd got out onto the chilly platform, they had disappeared.

Wherever he looked, unreal faces stared him out. The wind from the departing train shuffled them like cards.

It was a game of patience he couldn't win. For a moment he leaned against the wall, trying to gather his thoughts. The sky had clouded over, and the light was draining back into the sun. He tried to read the timetable to find out when the next train was due. Then he realised where his parents and sister must have gone. Trying to keep his mind clear, he walked through the ticket barrier and past the taxi rank just as the streetlamps were coming on, their light grainy with mist. The traffic sounded like a perpetual and vacant laughter.

Up the hill, past the school and the car park. Shops and offices gave way to houses with security lights that flashed on as Jason passed. Then the hospital, a series of grey buildings with grass verges surrounded by razor-wire. His parents' house was on the far side of the park. He'd been this way many times before. Just inside the gates, some children were playing on a climbing-frame made of scaffolding. A line of poplar trees flanked the pathway that divided the park into two areas – one neat and formal, the other uneven and wild. The dead leaves on the path must have fallen months ago.

Beyond the trees was a place he didn't recognise. Hints of light touched the gaps in the sky. The buildings ahead were formless and carried no signs. Tarpaulins hung from scaffolding like a huge window display. Jason walked faster, trying to recover his sense of direction. Telegraph wires made his scalp prickle as he turned around a corner, and found himself at the edge of a patch of waste ground which sloped down towards the town centre. He could see a blurred finger-painting of distant red and white lights against the night. The ground was littered with rusty cans and green glass. Some loose bricks suggested a past or future building site. Jason stared up into the clouds whose dirty grey stuck to the night like lichen. Suddenly he knew where to go.

It had been in his mind all the time, the only fixed point he had to rely on during that terrible Christmas at home. He was away from them now; their faces were blurred. Their voices couldn't reach him here, though the static in his head was almost as hard to endure. Not much further now. At the lower end of the waste ground, a gap in the wall let him through onto the railway line. The tunnel mouth was only a few yards ahead. Jason walked along the track until he couldn't see anything; then he lay down and put his head on the rail. The train took a long time coming. It always did.

THE CIRCUS FLOOR

It was nearly eight o'clock when Ian arrived at my room. I needn't have been worried, but it was force of habit by now to assume something was wrong when he was late. We sat together on the bed, our arms round each other. He explained to me that he'd spent half the day with a man he'd met the night before. He spoke looking away, then stared uneasily at me, his eyes shadowy and restless. 'Love you a lot,' he said. Last night he'd got home near four. Early in the morning his mother had woken him with the words 'Get up and pack your bags!' then gone to work; he hadn't been home since. 'She meant it even if she didn't mean it,' Ian said. He tried to kiss me, but I pushed my face past his and stared into the darkness over his shoulder. The impulse to leave him grew in me like an impersonal demand. He lay down and pulled me onto him; I kept still until he was asleep, then drew back. He was half curled on the bed like a child, in his usual clothes: loose jeans, striped shirt and rainbow braces. I sat and watched him sleep for an hour or more.

The tension in my chest hurt. I felt jealous and threatened; but somehow, beside that, I was gratified that Ian could fall asleep in my arms. Was I the safety net that he landed in whenever he fell off the trapeze? I thought of him as he usually was: always observing and reacting, never still. His mother had probably thought of him as a hyperactive child; now she thought of him as a delinquent. Ian was a changeling in her home: the residue of a failed marriage, troublesome because his life animated the past. For me, he was more like a conscience. He reminded me of battles unfought and pain unfelt. I stood up, touching the shoulder of his coat on the chair. Ian lifted his head and smiled up at me. 'Sorry to fall asleep on you,' he said. 'But you make me feel comfortable.' The electric fire was on, but there was a chilly draught from the window, where the catch was broken.

The night before, Ian must have been on form. That club was more his territory than mine. It brought him to life: he became vivacious, arch, with a grain of seriousness that made him compelling. The more he was admired, the more he felt the need to perform. Getting off with someone wasn't so much the goal as the applause. It took the sting out of the graceless confrontations he went through at home or in school. He'd act to me as well, but then he'd break up and confuse all of the roles at once, working towards the point of not acting. So I got all the pieces of the mosaic: the brilliant talker, the violent rebel, the bitter queen and the injured child. That assembly had to do, for want of a whole. My task was somehow to make them all live together.

I had been with him at times when all of his creations had fallen through. A few weeks before, he'd taken me to a park near his home; we sat down on a bench overlooking an ornamental garden. The only light came from two streetlamps on the far side. It was raining heavily; Ian clung to me, shivering. 'I've been coming here since I was a child,' he said. 'It's still the same. Nothing ever changes.' He began to cry; his chest was shaking, and the muscles in his face were rigid. 'Leave me. You won't see me again. Stay away, keep out of trouble.' His teeth started chattering, and he gave up the attempt to speak. I stayed with him, for what that was worth. At times like that Ian was completely alone. Worse than alone – he wasn't even a presence; he didn't even have himself to talk to. The chill and the darkness went through him like he wasn't there. Afterwards, the old Ian came back in bits and pieces, the house filling up one room at a time.

Towards ten o'clock I made Ian a cup of coffee and shook him awake. His arm felt cold, and he was trembling. 'It's freezing in here,' he said unsteadily. He had poor circulation, the effect of a heart weakened by persistent solvent sniffing in his early teens. The moisture in his eyes caught the light. His fear of going home was obvious; he wanted to lie here, protected. But I didn't want to touch him that night after what had happened during the day. When he'd put his coat on I suddenly embraced and kissed him, all the force of memory and fearful affection giving me the means to forget. 'Thank you,' he said quietly. Was he really as naive and dependent as that? No doubt it was a role like any other; but like all the others, it was compulsive, and meant at the time.

We walked up to the bus stop in town. The streets were crowded with young people coming out of the pubs. Couples were kissing in doorways and bus shelters. Men stopped to urinate in any dark place they could find. Ian talked about the man he'd been with. 'I'll always come back to you,' he said. 'You know that, don't you?' As we waited for the bus, he pointed into the grass bank beside a subway entrance. 'Look there.' A mouse, or a small rat, was leading several of its progeny up the slope. 'You never notice things like that, do you?' We arranged to meet at the weekend. I wished him good luck when he got home. 'I'm used to war,' he said with a comfortless smile.

Ian waved goodbye through the window at the back of the bus. I watched the bus dwindling in the long view downhill, past the unlit bulks of hotels and warehouses. This was the area where he and I belonged, in transition between the city centre and the suburbs. It was an area made up of derelict buildings, factories, car parks, railway bridges, subways, canals. An area given back to whatever of nature could improvise a living there. An area whose chief landmarks were half-concealed places that had the feel of the past, but were too anonymous to count as history. Ian knew these places, and brought them to life for me. It felt like remembering my own past. I walked home across the sawdust on the circus floor, out of reach of the lights; making my way among temporary structures of scaffolding and canvas, while the trapeze artists danced in mid-air overhead.

PLAYING DEAD

Ten years later, he went back again. This time he drove all the way from Exeter, changing from one motorway to another somewhere near Birmingham. It was Good Friday, and the roads were clotted with traffic. Rain, blown almost horizontal, crackled around the car like static electricity. Sunlight flickered occasionally on the wet road, dazzling him. On the edge of Cheshire, he pulled into a service station and sat there for an hour, fighting his reluctance to complete the journey. Alex wasn't sure what had kept him away, nor what he hoped to prove by returning. A pointless sense of guilt was hardening in him.

Had one stupid newspaper article really been enough to exile him from his home town? He wanted to believe that, but couldn't. The Little Chef was packed with edgy families hiding from the rain. Their arguments brushed him like wavebands: *Do what your father says. It's your fault, Darren.*

Now you'll be sulking all weekend. Alex stared at the window: thin, shimmering nets folded themselves down over the trees. Eventually, he got up and went back to his slightly rusty Volvo. And drove on, through a landscape that slowly awakened from the city. The clouds were edged with light. The trees stretched and shook themselves. The hillsides were a collage of green and yellow blotches, joined by perspective. Sunlight warmed his face; but the air was cold.

He reached Slateheath around four o'clock. On the cassette deck in the car, Neil Finn was singing about the dust from a distant sun. Everything here was much as he'd remembered it: the old church and streets of terraced houses, the new supermarket and glass-covered shopping arcade. In the town square, traders were still flogging imperfect clothes and reject china from little temporary stalls. Horror paperbacks, seventies rock albums, framed prints of children with tear-stained faces. He drove on through the narrow streets, past thin houses with unpainted doors and building sites that waved flags of tarpaulin. Nearly every street had a sign warning drivers to look out for blind people crossing. But it didn't sink in until he came to the junior school on the far side of town, the school he'd gone to three decades before. He noticed it had been rebuilt, though the playground was the same. Then two children with white sticks crossed the road in front of him, holding hands.

Alex drove back into the town centre, parked and sat there for half an hour, watching the street. At least a dozen blind people passed by in that time. A few wore dark glasses, and they all carried sticks; but only one, a young woman, had a guide dog. The interior of the car quickly became cold. Rain tapped out skeletal riffs on the windscreen. *Jesus*, he thought. No news wasn't always good news. The longer he sat there, on a street he'd walked down thousands of times as a child, the less he felt at home. All the blind people he'd seen here were younger than him. A flock of starlings jittered above the rooftops, tracing the wind's shape. Alex turned the key in the Volvo's ignition. No response. *Fuck*. He tried again and felt the car shudder to life.

The light was already fading as he drove to Alderley Edge. Factories were swollen with darkness. Some major companies had buildings out here; their private grounds included lakes and woodland. The roadway was lined with huge trees. A few shapeless crows' nests hung in their branches, like blood clots. Alex felt sleep waiting to catch him. He'd been driving all day. Just as the pattern of white trees against a black sky began to seem invariable, the road sloped sharply upwards; and there, past the next corner, was the Edge Hotel. It stood alone, looking out over a sea of parked cars to the long wooded slope that Alex supposed must be National Trust property. A rush of vertigo made him feel weightless, detached from the world.

He remembered going to a party somewhere near here as a teenager. There'd been no one to give him a lift home, and he was too self-conscious to crash out on the floor. So he'd walked home, a good six or seven miles as the crow flies. It was after midnight. Too drunk to follow the main road, he'd walked down through the Edge and tried to read the unlit road signs. He still remembered the cluster of distant streetlights. How he'd wanted to get lost and not get lost at the same time. How the trees had seemed like webs of darkness, veins from which darkness could be picked. Alex suddenly wished he'd stayed at the party. He might have got off with someone. Would it have made any difference? He remembered the last time he'd stayed at this hotel. Looking at the dark face of the building, he tried to remember what room they'd put him in. Then a sudden burst of sunlight made all the windows flare, like cameras pointed at him.

At least the hotel staff didn't appear to recognise his name. The room he'd booked turned out to be on the third floor. He followed the assistant up a spiral staircase that made him think of Polanski's *The Tenant*. Signed photographs of actors stared down from the walls; most were a few decades old. His room overlooked the Edge. From this height, the car park was like a cobbled street. Night seemed to fall as he stood looking out the window. He drew the curtains and, a minute later, heard the scratching of rain against the glass. It was strange how fatigue could distort time. A moment could stretch out forever; an hour could go past and you wouldn't notice.

By nine o'clock, the bar was crowded. Everyone from ageing long-stay residents to local teenagers whose eyes were wet with beer and frustration. Kurt Cobain screamed from the jukebox. It was funny how, to the children of those who'd been young in the sixties, the generation gap seemed to hurt as much as ever. And it wasn't just noise; even Alex, at forty, could hear that. It was pain. Too uneasy to sit still, he wandered through the semicircle of bars on the hotel's ground floor. There was a quiet lounge at one end, the air hazy with cigarette smoke. A dark-haired woman was sitting at the bar. When Alex bought a pint, she glanced at him. Her eyes were ringed with mascara, an old fashion that seemed to be coming back. He risked a brief smile. She smiled back, with an ease that seemed faintly sardonic. Under the make-up, her skin was very pale. She wasn't young; probably about his age. That was good, it made him feel safer.

'Hello,' she said. 'Haven't seen you here before.' He explained that he was on holiday, revisiting his home town. It had been a while. And her? 'I'm staying here, for the time being. Which may not be very long. We'll see.' Cursing his lack of originality, he asked: 'Are you here on your own?' She closed her eyes, then looked straight at him. 'Isn't everyone?' she said. Her eyes were like wounds. Alex couldn't look away. He bought her a drink – neat vodka on ice – and they sat down at one of the little tables by the far wall. Her name was Christine. She was from further north, near Middlesbrough; but her voice was unaccented and strangely lacking in emphasis. Her fingers on the narrow glass were as tight as wire. What was it about this place that always made him desperate for company? Perhaps it was affecting her in the same way.

Later, when they were drinking in the residents' bar, he told her about the last time. 'I was a journalist then. I'd come back to Slateheath a few times to visit my parents, before they moved away. And one time I noticed there seemed to be a lot of blind people in the town. Mostly young. More than when I'd been growing up there. Do you know anything about that, Christine?' She shook her head. 'Well anyway, I was working for a newspaper in Buxton. So I started to make enquiries. Nobody seemed to know anything. Not the council, the hospitals, my family or whoever. I couldn't even find out how many cases of blindness there were in Slateheath. Then someone at work said they'd heard a rumour about the new chemicals factory on the edge of the town, that it was linked to the Ministry of Defence. I went down to Slateheath and counted how many blind people there were on the streets. I saw thirty in an afternoon. Tried talking to a few of them, but they wouldn't say anything about what had happened. The only thing I was told, and at least three people said this, was that they'd lost their sight a long time ago.'

Alex kept his voice down, though the bar was nearly empty. A few loners were slumped on the comfortable settees or wandering through, presumably in search of a jukebox that would play 'Two Out Of Three Ain't Bad' – or failing that, 'Desperado'. The barman was polishing glasses while talking to one of the uniformed security men. Christine was sitting with her jaw propped in her hands. She looked younger and more relaxed than before. Perhaps because she was drunk. Alex wondered how much to tell her. 'Anyway,' he went on, 'the local health department refused to give me any information. So I went back to Slateheath and spent a day in the local library, reading the last few years' newspapers. A few adverts for talking books and Braille magazines, but no relevant stories. By then I was feeling a bit uncomfortable in the town. So I came here for the night. And I met someone. Just a girl, really. About eighteen, very friendly. And, well, she stayed with me.' Alex glanced at Christine's face; but she didn't react. 'There was some kind of party going on, and this bloke was taking photographs. He snapped one of me and Sally. I thought nothing of it. You know?

'A few days later, I wrote a story for the Buxton *Echo* called "What's Gone Wrong in Slateheath?" It said there was an epidemic of blindness, possibly linked to industrial pollution, and called for a public health enquiry. Three days after that, I was out of a job. The Slateheath *Daily Record* ran a front-page story on me as some kind of local outcast. They said I'd left the town because of trouble, like I was running away. And now I'd come back to make up stories and harm the town's image.' Alex clenched his fist. Christine touched the back of his hand. He gripped both her hands gently and kissed them. 'That wasn't all. They printed a picture of me and Sally. They said she was the local tart and I knew it. Christine, all I can say is, she might have been a prostitute, but if so it wasn't me who was paying her.

'That was the main thing the *Echo* sacked me for. That picture. I cleared my desk and went home to my flat. The lock was broken. Inside, everything was destroyed. Pictures smashed, books torn up, letters burned. They'd even taken all my LPs out of their sleeves and cracked them with a hammer.' Alex shut his eyes. He felt Christine's hand on his cheek, then her lips brushing against his. 'That was it. I felt they'd removed my background. Destroyed my past. What happened in Slateheath didn't concern me any more. I moved down to Exeter, got a job working with computers.' He opened his eyes; but the darkness stayed.

'Why have you come back?'

'I don't know. For me, I suppose. Not for the story. This is personal.' He stared at her, feeling an urge to say something foolish and drunken like *You're the only person who understands me*. By now, they were both drinking whisky; and she was smoking Marlboros, which he quite liked. Passive smoking was an old fetish of his. He'd almost forgotten about it in recent years.

Christine stared back at him. 'It's personal for me too,' she said. 'I mean, I'm not after anybody's money. But I don't know...' She stopped, drew on the fag-end of her cigarette and stubbed it out. The air in front of her face trembled. 'Jack, my husband, left me six years ago. My daughter Robin is in Manchester somewhere. I never hear from her. Five years ago, I was treated for severe depression. Privately. If I'd relied on the NHS, I'd probably still be in an institution. Everything has a price.' She drew closer to Alex, gripped his arm and whispered, 'Kiss me.' Her mouth tasted of smoke. He put one hand on the back of her neck, and brushed her hair back over her collar. Her tongue moved in his mouth as though she were trying to speak.

They went up to Christine's room on the second floor. It was well after midnight. Rain prickled the window. The air was dry and rather stuffy, with a faint clinical odour of pine disinfectant. While Christine brushed her teeth, he lay back on the bed and tried to relax. The freshly painted ceiling made him wonder what cracks or blotches had been covered up. By now, his fatigue had become a sort of aimless tension. If he'd been on his own, he would have stayed up drinking. Sometimes the main reason for sleeping with someone was to sleep. Christine came to the bed still dressed; he reached up for her. She massaged his neck and shoulders, but her hands were more tense than him.

In bed, they clung together as if the soft mattress could drown them. Alex came too quickly, but kept going until he felt Christine give a final, violent shudder and then lie still. Her fingers seemed to be fused to his shoulder blades. Afterwards, she switched on the bedside lamp and lit a cigarette. 'Do you mind me smoking in bed?' she asked. He shook his head. 'Not at all. I like smoke. Don't know why.'

'Because you're strange.' She looked at him, smiling. In the half-light her face was like a mask over darkness. Alex lay back and felt sleep blur the edges of the frame. They talked about music. Christine's ex-husband was a clarinet player, and she had a collection of bebop jazz records going back forty years. Alex told her about the sixties rock and folk albums the vandals had smashed. He'd managed to replace about half of them. The temperature in the room was falling; the central heating must have switched itself off, and the last few nights had been very cold. Alex pulled at the duvet, which was crumpled around their feet. 'Let's cover up.' Instead, Christine leaned over him and inhaled from the orange bud of her cigarette; then, gently, she breathed smoke over his face. He gripped her arms and pulled her down onto him.

The second time they made love, Alex didn't seem to climax – just to go from trying to being spent. He scarcely had time to remove the condom before the long-delayed sleep filled in his thoughts like a tide of coal dust. When he awoke, it was still dark. He was standing on some kind of tiled surface that chilled his bare feet. In front of him was a sheet of frosted glass which was grey, lit by something beyond. His hands were numb. Then they started to hurt.

Too frightened to scream, Alex reached for a light switch. His right hand touched a cord, but couldn't grip. He caught the end between two fingers and pulled. It was just an ordinary bathroom with a toilet and shower cubicle, painted in grey and white. The only bright colour was the red on his hands and in the washbasin. For a moment he was unable to move. Then he made himself go and look. There was nothing in the basin but a few pieces of broken glass and some blood which, from the cuts on his hands, was most likely his own. He must have smashed a wine glass. More blood was running down his arms, splashing on his feet. He was naked. The cuts weren't deep. It looked like he'd picked up a handful of broken glass and then used one piece to slash blindly at his left wrist, making three or four gashes but missing the artery.

Moving slowly and deliberately, he soaked a cloth in water and tied it round his left wrist. Then he unravelled a length of toilet paper and balled it in his damaged right hand. The pain made him feel separate from reality. In the next room, Christine was still asleep. He could hear her breathing, but he still pressed the light switch to check that she was unharmed. Then he realised he'd have to dress. He tried not to smear blood on his favourite shirt, but failed. Before leaving, he put a note on the bedside table. *Dear Christine, Had a small accident – I poured myself a glass of water and broke the glass, cutting my hand. I'd better go to hospital to get it looked at. Sorry about the mess.* He paused, then added, *I'll be in the hotel tonight. Hope to see you then. Alex.*

Downstairs, he gave the same story to the nightwatchman, who called a taxi and told him to go to the hospital in Slateheath. Alex almost decided not to bother, but he needed to be able to drive home on Monday. With only one dim light and an array of framed pictures, the hotel foyer was like a *film noir* setting. Daylight broke while he was on the way to Slateheath, on the long straight road that was lined with trees. Out here, the dawn chorus was so loud it was almost threatening. He could see magpies and crows perched in upper branches, and many smaller birds fluttering around the telegraph wires. The sun was a pale disc, not much brighter than the moon.

Alex was in casualty for two hours. There were quite a few people ahead of him: bruised and slashed faces, broken hands and jaws. A teenage boy's eye was swollen like a poached egg, weeping albumen. This was a strange time of day to get so many injured people. But Alex had heard that small towns were often more violent than cities. It always made him angry when the government used the increase in violent crime over the last ten years to argue that its own social policies were the necessary solution. As if the last decade itself had nothing to do with the problem. How long could they go on blaming liberal parents? If nothing changed, then soon they'd have to blame liberal grandparents. The nurse calling his name interrupted this train of thought. She swabbed his wounds with a disinfectant that stung bitterly, bandaged his right hand and put five stitches in his left wrist. When he said that he was here on holiday, she said 'Next time go to Aberystwyth.' He suspected he was being got at, and didn't want to pursue the point.

When he left the hospital, a kind of feathery sleet was falling. Gusts of wind blew it in all directions. Alex wasn't wearing a coat. He walked quickly to the coach station, which didn't seem to have changed since he was a teenager. His face felt stiff after last night's drinking, and some muscles he didn't often use ached at the pit of his stomach. It was a relief to get onto the coach. As he sat down, movement at the back of the station caught his eye. Two youths had pinned a third to the wall and were slowly aiming punches at him, mostly to the body. The victim didn't move: he stood between blows as if tied there. But they weren't holding him; why didn't he run? Why didn't anyone else intervene? There were people all around, but no one had reacted. As the coach started to pull out of the station, Alex saw the victim's face clearly. His eyes were dead white, unfocused. Alex suddenly realised that the boy wasn't moving because he couldn't see where was safe to go, or how many people were attacking him.

On the road back to Alderley Edge, the sleet became a sudden hailstorm. It beat against the coach windows in a sharp percussive frenzy, like a thousand heads vomiting their own teeth. The green fields were streaked with glittering white. After a few minutes, it stopped; the sun came out. When Alex got off the coach, he scooped up a few hailstones with his left hand. They shone like glass pebbles rounded by the sea. Then they melted, ran together, and left only wetness and a few specks of some blackish-grey deposit.

Alex got back to the Edge Hotel in time for a late breakfast. Christine was nowhere in sight; he didn't know her room number. His own room was just as he'd left it, except that the curtains were open. He looked down through the window at the green and brown slope of Alderley Edge, blurred with light like a fresh painting. Between him and the view was his own reflection, as faint as a shadow. A buried memory drifted upwards, close to the surface; then fell again. He walked around the room and the attached bathroom, checking that no blade or breakable glass object was within easy reach. Then he lay down and went to sleep.

That evening, he saw Christine in the bar. 'Are you all right?' she said. 'I was really worried.' Her eyes sparkled with a strange kind of irony. Because she was glad to see him, or not? Remembering the broken glass incident, he felt uneasy in her company. But apart from asking how he was, she didn't try to probe. He told her about the hospital and the incident at the coach station. 'I just wish… I could really see what's happening. What's behind it. Then I might be able to do something.'

She gripped his left hand, the one that wasn't bandaged. 'Don't worry. The town will make you see.' But all his life, Alex realised, he'd associated Slateheath with narrow views and reduced horizons. It wasn't just the people, it was the way the place looked: the uniform streets, the way sunlight never seemed to reach the pavement. For him, 'outside' had never meant outside the house; it meant outside the town. How could he explain that to Christine? It was easier to rest his head on her shoulder, squeeze her hand, let her fetch the drinks. He was still very tired; and as he started to get drunk, the feeling came back that he'd already seen the truth. If only he could remember it.

Later, he took off the bandages. His right hand was still raw, but the wounds had closed. The stitches in his left wrist gleamed like fillings. This time they were in his room; Christine was waiting in the bed. When he joined her, she slipped over him and reached to turn out the light. They made love slowly, Christine doing most of the work. As he started to come, Alex ran his hands down her back and felt her sweat sting them. Her hair was in his mouth. For a few precious minutes, he didn't feel scared. Then he fell asleep.

The first thing he knew was a bitter taste in his mouth. There was a glass in his left hand. It wasn't broken. It wasn't empty. The carpet tickled his feet. Not far away, he could hear the sound of Christine's regular breathing. He was not in pain. Even the ache where he'd cut himself was gone. He felt his way along the wall to the light switch. The glass in his hand was half full of water. On the dressing table was a small brown bottle, the kind you kept pills in. Like the pills scattered around it, red with a black stripe.

He took a step nearer to the bed. Then another. The tempo of Christine's breathing remained the same, but its depth increased. 'Stop pretending to be asleep,' he said. She looked up at him, her face devoid of expression. 'How many did I take?' he asked. 'How fucking many? Tell me.'

Christine shrugged. 'One or two. You'll live.' She started to climb out of the bed. 'Alex, I'm sorry—'

'You what? You fucking knew. Maybe not the first time, but tonight. Or how many others have you killed?'

She shook her head. 'They don't die. The attempts fail. Just like mine.' She was crying. Alex stepped towards her, clenched his fist and swung it backwards into her face. 'You parasite,' he said quietly. 'You sick monster. You *fucking bitch*.' She put her hand to her mouth; it came away bloody. Her face was trembling like a paper lantern in the wind. He looked in her eyes and saw only darkness, as if her eyes weren't there. Something clicked in his mind. 'Christine,' he said. He gripped her arms and leant towards her. She didn't move. Then her face was against his chest and her crying echoed inside him. 'Christine, I'm sorry.' He wrapped his arms around her and sat down on the bed. They kissed gently, with a mutual caution. 'I need you to come with me,' he said.

Rain was falling quietly from the blue-grey velvet of the night sky. The trees to either side were hardly visible. They'd gone from the road onto the network of footpaths that criss-crossed the Edge. Alex knew the way. Christine was just behind him, and it somehow helped. He couldn't do this alone. 'I don't know how old I was,' he said. 'Maybe six or seven. One day I ran away from home. Didn't get very far. My parents were screaming at each other. It happened a lot when I was little. I think that was the day my mum threw a bottle at my dad and it broke the living-room window. I ran out into the street and just kept going, until I was out of the town. I came up here. I thought if I came out of the Edge with my clothes in rags and said I didn't have a name, whoever found me would have to look after me.

'I found this pool with trees and bushes all round it, next to a quarry that was half filled in with rocks. I'd been running, and I splashed some water over my face to cool down. I remember breaking my reflection and watching it re-form, and wondering if it was my reflection or my shadow. Then I heard some people shouting. The sound of twigs breaking and heavy footsteps. Then a man came running towards the pool. He looked about nineteen. There was blood on his face. When he saw me, he stopped and turned away. He'd got to the edge of the quarry when the others caught him. Six or seven men, about the same age. They didn't see me. I watched them circle round him and then close in. He tried to break away, but one of them tripped him. Then they kicked him to death. After a few minutes, they stopped. One of them said something like *That's it, the show's over. Nothing really happened*. And one of the others said *Nothing ever does*.

'After they'd gone, I crouched there for more than an hour. The sun was shining through the trees. The blood on the ground dried out, went from red to almost black. I knew he was dead, but I had to make sure.' Alex paused. He was standing still. Christine was beside him, her face in shadow. They were very near to the place, and he had to finish his

197

story before going on. 'From the way his body was lying, I could tell most of the bones were broken. There was a crow perched on a rock by the side of his face. I saw it pecking into his throat. It had already taken his eyes. I turned away and started running down the slope, towards home. It was a long way, but I didn't slow down. Those blank sockets were staring in my head. I never told anyone. A couple of weeks later, they found him. The killers probably still live here. I never ran away from home.' Christine touched his face; he didn't know if the wetness was tears or sweat. They walked on in silence.

It was beginning to get light when they reached the quarry. The surface of jagged rocks was only a few feet below ground level. The pool, several yards away, was still reflecting the night sky. In between, the ground was soft and uneven. A high, broken chorus jarred the still air. Christine looked at Alex. He nodded, wanting to hold her but feeling somehow exposed. A few paler fragments shone from the dark earth at his feet. Were they only rocks? He knelt down to examine them. Then Christine said, 'My God. Look.'

Some people were walking through the trees towards them, slowly. They stumbled and walked into branches, making no effort to protect themselves; but somehow, they kept their balance. At first, Alex thought they were sleep-walking. Then he realised they were blind. Christine gripped his arm; he didn't know if she was trying to reassure him or herself. More and more of them appeared, spreading out in a rough circle to enclose the pool, the quarry and the space in between. It was daylight now, but the trees and bushes were still black. Further down the slope, the slow procession continued. There were hundreds of them. Alex stood up, and felt something shift gently under his feet. All around him the ground was rippling and swelling, about to break. A crow or a magpie screamed from beyond the pool. He looked at the ring of blank faces, and began to realise how they would make him see.

Christine moved away from him. She walked into the crowd; they let her pass through. Had they used her, or would it have happened anyway? It didn't seem to matter now. Kneeling again, he thrust his hands into the loose soil. He felt something warm. Then the ground exploded, and the air was full of birds. They looked like starlings. Dirt rained from their wings. They rose in a cloud, then settled onto him. He felt their beaks strike his face, his neck, his hands. They stabbed through the cloth of his shirt. He was unable to move as his eyes were pecked out, one after the other. The world became a red blur. And then he could see. All the wounds were eyes. The light poured into him, filling him like wine in an empty glass. He could see all the others, gathered round the quarry's white eye and the pool's black eye. Just watching. Not moving. Their faces looked grey and brittle, like a crowd photo in an old newspaper. Beyond them, he could see the fixed structures of the town and his own past. And still he felt no pain. Only a terrible sadness that a ritual could use so much power and achieve so little.

THE EARTH WIRE

Geoff's first encounter with the unknown had been when he found his parents' house burned out, and the street already in the process of demolition. He hadn't known what to expect, of course, returning so soon after the disturbances. The area hadn't changed that much. It was north of Birmingham, part of the confusion of little towns and industrial wasteland that was still called the Black Country, after the factory-based conurbation of the old days. The old communities had declined with the closure of the small industries, mostly car-related, that had formed their ground. In spite of projects of redevelopment, no new imprint had really taken hold. Asian small businesses had filled a few of the economic and territorial gaps, like metal in a decaying line of teeth. The present landscape was a mosaic of elements juxtaposed without any kind of underlying pattern. In the gaps, the traces of the past were still visible: the network of disused canals and railways, dating from the Industrial Revolution.

This much, Geoff had grown up with, and observed on his intermittent visits home over the past seven years. It still made him feel lost, a prisoner of his own adolescence. Even when away, he could sense himself picking through the same jigsaw of pieces that didn't fit together. After the disturbances he'd felt compelled to visit his parents, if only to confirm that that part of his life was still in place. It wouldn't be long before the postal and telephone services were put back to rights, but in the meantime all he could do was take the train up from Surrey. Living in the countryside, he'd escaped the worst of the past few months. London, Birmingham and the North had been most badly affected, he knew. The imposition of martial law had coincided with a breakdown of general order. In other major cities, riots had turned into open civil warfare. Now, according to the newspapers, order had been restored; but many travel routes and communications were blocked off. In isolated districts, violence between gangs was still escalating. Meanwhile, the majority of peaceful citizens had gone back to work, waiting for news of the international situation.

On the train, Geoff had been unnerved by the silent young men in green uniforms who restlessly patrolled the carriages for want of anything else to do. From their faces, you might have thought they were outlaws, not soldiers. But most people looked like that these days; it came from living on your nerves, not knowing what or who could be counted on. Near home, the recent disorder was visible in details: smashed windows, wrecked cars, shops boarded up. Soldiers or armed police stood in little groups on street corners or traffic islands, watching. There was little activity in the streets; it was a Sunday morning in January, still and clear.

On the corner opposite the street where Geoff had been born, a chorus of massed voices sounded from the little church with its metallic Christ nailed to a concrete slab. He couldn't remember that place ever having had much of a congregation. Its narrow stained-glass windows were protected by wire grids. The voices divided into nervous fragments before unifying for another phase of certainty. As Geoff walked away, the reality filled his view before his mind could make sense of it. The street opposite was mostly burned down. His parents' house was just recognisable, a hulk of carbon boarded up against the daylight. The door and its number were gone. The street was being systematically demolished from the far end; for now, the machines stood idle, seeming too large for the fragile structures they were intended to bring down.

Geoff walked back to the church and let the communal voice fill his head for a few moments. Then he went back down the road, checking its name, confirming that his parents' home was among those burned out, even if he'd misidentified the building itself. Beyond the demolition machines, two lines of shops pointed back towards the town centre. From that direction, an old man was walking an Alsatian along the road; Geoff greeted him. 'Do you know what happened up there in Tulson Road?' he asked.

'There was a fire,' was the answer. 'Don't know how. That was in November, you know. When all the trouble was. Nothing could get through the bloody roads, with all the crowds and the fighting. Could have been that that started it. A petrol bomb. Or the Army trying to show who was boss. Only kids, half of them.'

'Were many people killed?' Geoff thought of the silent Christmas that had followed the uprisings, most of the postal service suspended. There was no reliable way of getting in touch with anyone in the cities, and snowstorms made all the travel problems worse. People were said to have starved in some areas.

'You mean in the fire? Nobody took much notice at the time. I think they evacuated most of the houses, though. But God knows where they can all have ended up. In those Army hostels you read about now, maybe. Why, you from round here?'

'Yes,' Geoff said. 'My parents lived in Tulson Road. Their house is gone.'

The old man stared at him, as if really seeing him for the first time. 'That's a shame. They could still be around, you know. You want to make enquiries. Try some of the hospitals, maybe. They wouldn't be there any more, but you might be able to trace them. Good luck.' The Alsatian edged past Geoff suspiciously and accompanied his owner towards what remained of Tulson Road. Geoff headed back into the town centre. But the further he walked, the more his own past seemed to detach itself from him. It was all at the edge of his vision, coming apart, instead of being part of himself. The landscape itself felt unreal and enclosed on its own hidden purposes. Advertising boards screened off patches of wasteland; posters claimed the walls of derelict buildings. He walked around the town centre for an hour, unable to convince himself that he'd once lived here.

At the end of the morning, people emerged from the churches and disappeared into their homes. Nobody was even playing football in the park. Geoff walked past the line of poplar trees there, held onto the railings and looked over the expanse of thin grass that was lightly tinted with frost. He wished he could take cover inside his own childhood. He'd never felt lost then.

The same impulse directed him onto the canal system, an endless stony network that led nowhere but onto renewed outgrowths of itself. At least there were no soldiers here. The towpath was narrowed by railings, factory walls and rough, impassable slopes; the water was dark and static, reflecting nothing. Here and there a few thin patches of ice hardened the surface. Geoff wandered in a vague, purposeless state through dirty stone tunnels and over small iron bridges. Eventually, that stretch of canal ended at a wooden lock. Above this, a boy was standing on a footbridge and looking down onto half a mile or so of water. Geoff climbed up to share the view. He felt weary and confused. It was mid-afternoon and he hadn't eaten since morning. That, and a hint of the coming darkness, made the canal below appear black and without limit, a gap in the world.

The youth was looking at him. He was about seventeen, of average height and build, wearing black jeans and a waterproof grey jacket with a zip. He looked vaguely familiar, perhaps like someone Geoff had been at school with. His hair was black and cropped short but unevenly; his face was pale, as though he were unused to daylight. 'You're in trouble, aren't you?' he said. Geoff gazed down at the water. The wooden handrail of the bridge shook as he leant on it. He looked back; the boy's face held a complex burden of patience and sadness. His eyes were an unusually deep blue, the colour of stained glass. 'Why not talk to me?'

'What's been going on here?' Geoff said. 'I haven't been back here since all the trouble in November. My parents' house is burned down. I don't know where they are. But everything's upside down and I simply... don't know where to start. He pulled at the handrail as if he could tear it free as a weapon. His chest was shaking with a grief still locked in his body. His face tightened, but only the cold reached it and there was no feeling of relief, only the annoyance of having lost his self-control in front of a stranger.

'Look,' the boy said, 'I can tell you something about how things have gone here. Maybe I can help you reconnect yourself. All I do these days is watch and listen. And talk to people. I've lost my parents, too. They died three years ago. I live in their flat, partly. And partly on the canal, in a boat. That's where I sleep. It's out of harm's way... You look like you've been awake all night. Did you just get here today?'

'Yes, this morning. I've been walking around for hours. I'll have to go back. Can't stay at my parents', can I?'

The boy thought for a moment. 'I'll take you round to the flat. You can sit down there and talk for a bit. I'll find you something to eat. You look hungry. My name's Mark, by the way.' He led Geoff downhill onto a crowded estate of little terraced houses, a few decades old. Mark's house was shadowed by the house facing it; it had an air of preserved age which it no doubt owed to the perpetual lack of light. His flat was the upper floor of the house; the stairs began a few feet back from the front door. 'You can't really tell what's new and what's old round here, can you?' Mark said. 'Whatever they build turns just like everything else in a few years.'

Upstairs it was cold and dim. 'There's no electric here,' Mark explained. 'I use batteries for most things – radio, torch, clock. There's a paraffin cooker here, and a heater on the boat. Otherwise nothing.' He coughed. The floor was scattered with bits of electrical circuits: wires, batteries, fuses and less identifiable components. 'That's my hobby. I mend radios, things like that. I used to have a Citizens' Band radio. But everything like that has been outlawed now. So I'm trying to fix the radio on my boat to pick up stray frequencies. I lie there at night, wandering over the airwaves. Listening for all the drifting voices of the lost ones.' He struck a match and lit the paraffin stove in the corner of the room. Its bluish light circled his dark head for a moment like an aura.

Geoff sat in a dusty chair and fought off all the questions that clustered around him. He focused on the wavering cone of light: blue at its heart, then purple, mauve, flickering red at the edges. Mark's eyes were points of colour in a blurred face. He took off his coat; underneath, he was wearing a pale shirt and braces. His arms and hands were thin in proportion to his body. He carried on talking, evidently glad to have company, as he heated up a tin of soup. Geoff listened, bemused, to this voice that seemed to consist of a throng of submerged partial voices, that talked with and against itself.

The soup boiled; Mark poured it into a cup, drank a mouthful, and passed the rest to Geoff. 'Electricity is fascinating,' he was saying. 'It does almost everything in the city. People live by it, yet they've got no idea how it works. And it can do all kinds of damage as well. You'll probably see the Wheel tonight. But an electric current is like any kind of power. It has a natural tendency to hurt people.' He picked up a plug from the floorboards and opened it swiftly with a screwdriver. 'You know what the middle wire is? The earth wire. Right. The plug can work without it. It's just a safety device. The conscience of the circuit. True?' Geoff asked what the Wheel was. 'You'll know when you see it,' was the only answer.

The room darkened, shrinking around the flame of the stove. 'Some awful things are happening,' Mark said quietly. 'Give me time, I might understand them. I'm just a watcher and a listener. Nobody has any peace these days. Before the soldiers came in, there were gangs fighting the police. Now, there's like another army. Young people with no power, only a charge. And a need to hurt. They've called on resources no community should know about. I think all the things that kept people together have been turned against them. There's no community now. Only the mob. Anyone who's different gets… reversed. Made into carbon. Imagine shouting No, denying at the top of your voice. Then imagine *doing* that No to someone. Last, imagine *being* that No forever, all the way through.' The voice dissolved into a fit of coughing. Mark's body was contorted with the force of it.

When the boy looked up, his face was luminous with sweat. He pulled on his coat and zipped it up. 'Let's go,' he said. 'I'll show you where my boat is. We'll be there in time to see the Wheel.' Geoff stood up and followed Mark back downstairs and through the narrow streets towards the canal. By now, he was worried about Mark's condition as well as whatever they were going to witness. But the sense of displacement still clung to him, leaving him helpless. A single white streetlamp illuminated the stretch of canal where Mark's boat was moored, a few yards below road level. It was a short black barge with windows around a central cabin; navy blue curtains were drawn along the sides. Mark and Geoff climbed onto the barge and sat on the roof, waiting for it to stop rocking. By now, night was settling all around. In the lamplight, the ripples spreading on the canal surface looked like silver wires.

'I sleep here at night,' the boy said. 'It's quiet and peaceful out here. Just me and the radio, and the canal water transmitting the murmurs from the past. I keep lots of old things inside, by the bunk. Notebooks, photographs, tapes, newspapers. Everything I can remember, everything people tell me, ends up here.' They could see along the shining distance of still water to the next bridge; and to one side, the flaking wall of a disused factory. To the other side, a railway cutting fell down into the darkness. The streetlamp outlined the whitewashed metal footbridge that linked them to the road, several yards overhead; from below, it seemed too bright and delicate to be real.

Mark stared intently into the surrounding gloom. Could walk along here with you,' he muttered, 'and tell you who built everything, and when. How every bridge was designed, how they set the stones, who opened the factories and who shut them down. I heard a song about it once. You know it? Their mark on this land is still seen and still laid, the way for a commerce where vast fortunes were made. The supply of an Empire where the sun never set, which is now deep in darkness but the railway's there yet. It's true. This area's another residue where the glacier of profit stopped and melted a little before it passed on, a long time ago. If you lie here long enough, you can hear the stone and metal still going on about it.' His eyes were the same intense blue as the paraffin flame, dissolving into black at their centres.

Looking out onto the canal, as the last traces of daylight turned to iron, Geoff began to see a few unstable outlines. As they moved they took up light and became more complex, more nearly alive. They struggled and burned into figures. Now he could see men working on the bridges and the railway, opening the lock at the head of the canal, crowding out of the factory doors. Water poured into the canal from the open lock; waste flowed down from the channels in the factory wall. Off to the side, he could see women coming home from their jobs, cleaning and cooking in their houses; he could see children playing in the web of streets and throwing stones into the canal. There was something almost terrible in the intensity of this scene, composed as it was of grains of colour moving against the common darkness of water and sky. Geoff closed his eyes and heard the violent beating of his own heart.

In a few moments everything became quiet and still again. Geoff sat up, and felt the boat tremble. Mark was blinking into the lamplight, confused. 'God, that was a strange dream,' he murmured, and gripped Geoff's hand momentarily. 'We'll fall off here if we're not careful.' As clumsily as if the cold had got into their limbs, the two climbed down onto the towpath. Something slowed Geoff's movements and made him feel distant from this situation. Had he been able to find the words, he might have called it the possessive hold of memory, the way it resisted change. But it made no sense for him to feel like that about his parents, now of all times. Nor about Mark, when he'd only known him a few hours.

He needed to be alone for a minute, to regain his perspective. 'Do you want something to eat?' he asked the boy. Mark shook his head; he was busy fastening the boat's moorings. Geoff remembered passing a shop just up the road. 'Wait here,' he said. 'I'll be back in a few minutes.' Out of sight of the canal, he had a strange feeling of relief. The small chip shop had several other customers. A group of teenagers stood round a video game, one playing, the others watching. Geoff waited by the counter, reassured by the sense of anonymity. He could hear the distant contention of voices; they were in his head, he imagined, until he noticed the shop's owner looking past him at the window. The narrow street was filled with people. Hurriedly, the teenagers left the shop to join them. Geoff crossed to the glass door and looked out. They weren't soldiers, just a crowd of youths all going in the same direction. He could hear angry voices, but no chorus.

As rapidly as it had filled, the road emptied again. 'Where are they going?' Geoff asked. 'Who are they?' The Asian shop owner was still looking outward, not moving. The video game flashed and buzzed nervously. The pale strip light by the window superimposed the interior on the view. The darkness outside was an impersonal pressure that felt charged with threat.

'Over the canal,' the shop owner said at last. 'They're just a gang of hooligans. Or they were. There are more of them every day. I don't know why the soldiers don't stop them. The soldiers interfere in everything else.' He turned away and began stacking cans and boxes behind the counter. His hands were unsteady, but an effort of concentration kept him from knocking anything over. Geoff hoped the man wouldn't mind him leaving without buying anything. He had to catch up with the group. Mark would know what they were up to.

He got back to the canal just in time to see the last of the crowd disappearing along the towpath, under and around the bridge. Near his barge, Mark was sprawled at the water's edge. He'd fallen down; one of his hands gripped the metal ring that the mooring-rope was tied to. Geoff turned him over; he was breathing heavily, and bleeding from his mouth. His eyes opened. 'I'm all right,' he said. 'They knocked me over, that's all.' He coughed hard and sat up. There was mud on the arm and shoulder of his coat from the ground. He held onto Geoff's arm and pulled himself to his feet, then stood very still, as though he were about to fall again. His face was passive, lost to thoughts that nobody could share.

Then he knelt, dipped a hand in the murky water, and wiped the blood from his mouth. 'This is the Wheel,' he said. 'We can go and watch if you want. You ought to see it once.' Picking his way carefully in the poor light, he led Geoff along the towpath, then up into a maze of side-streets and bridges where the canal and railway network had been overlaid with a perpetuation of the town. More strongly than before, Geoff could feel the tension that the gang left in its wake – a stillness heavy with anger, like a cloud that was about to turn itself inside-out and discharge its secret violence in one flash. They caught up with the mob at a crossroads, where a valley in one plane coincided with a hilltop in another. His father would have called it a saddle-point, Geoff reflected.

There was rain in the air now, a vague drizzle that could be felt only when it settled against the skin, and seen only when it made the pavements reflect the lamplight. From a distance, Geoff and Mark watched the crowd of youths gather closer together at the crossroads. There were about a hundred of them; some were older than Geoff, some younger than Mark. There were women among them, though not many. The crowd would block off any traffic. But no soldiers or police came to break them up. They were completely quiet now, drawn towards some common purpose. Geoff's chest tightened as he saw that their focus was a prisoner: someone half-lifted in the middle of the gang, his arms held apart. His face was gagged, and a rope around his neck was being used to prevent him from struggling. Geoff pressed himself back in the shadow of the wall, trying to make himself smaller; and to make the image smaller, reduce it to a television screen, a photograph. The boy was silent beside him, watching.

On the far side of the crossroads, a wire fence had been torn down from in front of a power generator. Between the red DANGER sign and the two black tanks set in the ground, some kind of machine had been installed. As far as Geoff could see, it was a metal cross supported on a crude motor, which was connected to the generator by heavy black cables. Some of the crowd were chanting now, but out of unison; Geoff couldn't make out any of the words. Two men tied the prisoner to the iron cross, which was then tilted backwards to free it from the ground. Now he was suspended in mid-air, unable to move; his arms and legs were stretched out in a regular X. Throughout this process he had shown no sign of resistance. The nearest of the crowd to the centre drew back. A mist of raindrops hung in stasis between the sodium lamps and the pavement, increasing Geoff's sense of being witness to something detached from reality.

Everyone was looking at the helpless figure, directing their tension inward to the crossroads. Violence flickered in the air like dark moths; energy twitched the wires of falling rain. But nothing happened, and the mob were as passive as their victim. Then his gag started to burn. His face was obscured by smoke as the cross began turning. Sparks jumped between the limbs, hissing. Then the motor was coughing with life, and the cross was spinning into a blur of crimson and blue flame. The air became dense with the mixed odours of burning materials: rubber, paint, flesh and cloth. That and the drifting smoke made Geoff feel drugged to the point of insensitivity. The wheel dimmed, its blackened weight appearing massive as it stopped moving. The face was no longer distinct. Without a focus, the crowd drifted apart uneasily. Some of them stood as though lost, taken over by the night that pressed in from all directions.

In minutes, they had dispersed entirely, leaving only the outstretched figure that had formed the centre of the gathering. At a distance, what was visible looked like the negative image of one of Blake's angels. 'Who was it?' Geoff asked.

'Nobody,' the boy answered. 'Could have been anyone.' As they walked back towards the canal, he added: 'You'll see it again. Happens all the time now. But we saw it together. That means neither of us can go away and say he didn't see it. True?' When they reached the towpath, they were alone. Mark leaned on Geoff's arm for support. 'I need to rest a bit,' he said. They stopped at a bench lit from overhead. The rain had intensified, darkening their coats. Geoff held the boy's shoulders while he shook with a fit of coughing.

More than rain was visible in the air now. Ashes were blowing towards them across the canal, like creased snowflakes of carbon. Where they struck Geoff's face and hands they felt clinging, permanent. He felt as though his own core had been blackened, and the night had come in to claim all of his memories, his debts, his future. Mark was whispering something in a tired but urgent voice. 'It all goes on and on,' he was saying; 'the more you take in, the more gets taken out of you. I'm just a watcher and a listener... I can't change anything. I can't even tell you where to look, or who to go to. I'm losing myself, that's why... Nothing in my lungs but pollution and bad dreams.' His words dissolved into a kind of helpless choking; he pressed a handkerchief into his mouth. It came away deep red. That could be a disease or an internal wound; Geoff couldn't tell which.

A breeze caught the stained handkerchief and made it flutter. The rain diluted the blood, running it through the boy's fingers. The colour washed out with unnatural speed; within a minute the cloth was entirely white. Perhaps there was some active chemical in the rain. Or, Geoff realised, perhaps the blood wasn't as material as it looked. Mark clenched his fist. He was trembling with cold; his eyes stared at something in the distance. 'We ought to get you to a hospital,' Geoff said.

Mark shook his head and smiled briefly. 'Just get me back to the boat,' he said. 'I'll feel better when things have changed a little. You should understand that by now.' The strength was coming back into his voice. He leaned nearer to Geoff; close up, his eyes appeared blue-black, like bruises. 'But what are you going to do?' he asked. 'You still don't know where to start, do you? Everything you see here makes you want to run away. You see your parents everywhere, and instead of looking for them, you're looking for a way to get free of them. All you want is something else, somewhere else. Do you wonder you can't begin to work out what it is?'

Several minutes passed in silence. Mark's face seemed to undergo conflict from within; it gave way to a community of faces, old and young, male and female. Then he regained himself. 'Make contact somewhere,' he said quietly. 'If you give yourself up to everyone, you'll be torn apart. But if you hold off too long, you'll never be able to earth yourself. You're like a Catherine wheel, spinning instead of moving. True? Plug in somewhere, connect yourself.' He reached up and touched Geoff's cheek; a fragile pulse of warmth passed through his fingertips.

Soon after, Geoff was standing alone on the canal towpath, looking at the black barge with its curtains drawn against the lamplight. He'd helped Mark walk back to his boat and climb inside. As Geoff had last seen him, the boy was lying on his side in the narrow bunk, turning the knob on the radio endlessly back and forth in search of the wavelength by which the dead spoke. It was a small portable radio, run on batteries, and weakened by Mark's recurrent tinkering with its circuits. 'Be careful,' were Mark's final words to him. Geoff stood beside the still barge for an hour or more, knowing that he had no reason to stay.

When he began to walk, his limbs felt mechanical and foreign. The empty night stripped him of identifying features. Whatever had kept him waiting by the boat faded into the blur of thoughts that could not be remembered. In the distance, a few city lights shone yellow and silver. They looked nearer than they were. Geoff thought of the Wheel, flaming with all the vivid colours of terror and denial; and he thought of the red handkerchief whitening faster than a person could die. At the first bridge, he turned back and tried to make out the shape of the barge against the dark water. He fought off the impression that it was being carried away into the distance by water currents. This was a canal, not a river. Nothing moved here. Indeed, nothing much had changed here in a hundred years.

IN THE BRIGHTNESS OF MY DAY

In a room filled with clothes and old magazines, a blind cripple turned over in his sleep. The bus climbed the long hill towards the Northfield shopping centre. Moth sat on the upper deck, watching the sunlight painting in cracks in the evening sky. The clouds were like a bunch of roses, pink and gold and violet, flattened underneath by a sheet of glass. Soon the darkness would blotch them into nothing. On the High Street, the low sun flared across shop windows, obscuring their displays. The pavements were almost empty, but the roadway was charged with traffic. At the traffic lights, an old man walked slowly across the road, shadowed by his lack of energy. Moth watched the green man's image stutter and turn red. He took a steel nail-file from his jacket pocket and slowly whittled at the fingernails on his left hand.

It was a Friday evening late in May; the day had been cool and bright. By eight o'clock a white moon, frail as a projected image, shone almost full above the red-brick office blocks. Moth walked through the city centre, absorbing lights and voices. He was wearing a floral shirt with black sleeves. Above New Street, the upper storeys of hotels and shops displayed a complex, delicate stonework that reminded him of 1960s films. He watched a lot of old films on TV, late at night in his flat. Away from the main streets, everything became grey: closed offices, the hospital buildings, the law courts. Near Aston University, the walls around condemned buildings were plastered with several layers of posters advertising pop concerts or new records. Moth stopped in at the Triangle cinema to look at the programme for the new season. *Midnight Cowboy* was coming back in August. Still reading, he walked back into town, where it was getting dark. You noticed that more where the lights were bright.

The pub was below the ground, at the foot of a staircase which began at street level. Its bar-room was designed rather like an amphitheatre: the bar in the middle, an oval, and the tables near the walls all the way round. It meant that everyone could see everyone else, at least if they were standing. Moth waited in the shadow of the stairs, one elbow resting beside his drink on the jukebox. When there were no vacant seats at the tables or the bar, newcomers were forced to drift in the half-lit ring of open space, blinking at the smoke. Immobile, Moth let the confusion of voices and blurred faces resolve itself in his mind as a composite image, a mosaic. He drifted from one voice to another as though scanning frequencies on the radio. Two youths in evening suits brushed past him, one saying to the other: '… needed eight stitches. So I said to her, call *me* a size-queen, at least *my* eyes aren't bigger than my arsehole…' The voice caught in

Moth's thoughts like a fragment of broken glass. Darkness gripped his hands, draining strength from the fingers.

An hour later, someone bought Moth a drink. He was a nervous man in his mid-thirties, his forehead already on the way towards joining the back of his neck. 'I'm surprised you're on your own,' he said. As he spoke, he held his pint up to his mouth like a faulty microphone. His name was Glen, and he'd come up from Stoke for the weekend. Moth said he was a sixth-former who lived with his parents. Inwardly, he calculated that there was no point in taking this one back. He was too old for Matt. Moth asked Glen for his impression of Birmingham. 'Icy,' was the reply. 'All except you.' Moth smiled in his best angel manner. 'Well, I'll have to be going soon,' Glen said.

Moth touched his arm, as though brushing off a loose thread. 'I know somewhere we could go for a while.' Glen stared and nodded, then emptied his glass in one slow gulp. They pushed through the human traffic jam to the foot of the dark staircase. On the street corner, the queue outside a fish and chip shop merged with that outside a bus shelter. The last bus out of town turned a corner, empty and staring white like a face on a cinema screen. Moth led his catch in silence past the town hall and the cathedral, and through a stone maze of upper Hockley backstreets to where the roadway bridged an unlit stretch of canal. 'Down here. Quick.' There was a steep flight of metal steps leading down onto the towpath.

In the shadow of the bridge, three alcoves in the brick wall to either side were half-filled with rubble. Across the canal the back wall of a factory was composed of squares of corrugated iron bolted together. Moth lit a cigarette, to see better. The light glinted from bottles and fragments of glass on the heaps of shattered brick. He held Glen's head to kiss him, exhaling smoke into his mouth. Then he pushed the other man down onto his knees. No words were exchanged. Moth unfastened his jeans and then stood motionless, watching the minimal ripples of moonlight on the canal surface, so transient they could be hallucinatory. He thought: eyes never rest. Even in complete darkness, the random activity of nerves makes transient flickers of light appear on the retina. Matt often told him things about vision; it was his favourite subject.

Glen's head was moving back and forth in the darkness. Moth's left hand traced the side of Glen's face, down to the taut neck muscles. His fingernails were sharp as glass splinters, sharp as a broken mirror. He scratched Glen's throat, and felt blood flow. The head continued moving, regular as a wind-up doll. Moth imagined severing the blood vessels with his nails. The image was enough to bring him off. He drew back, fastened his zip and walked away. Glen, still kneeling, rubbed at his neck. 'Jesus Christ.' Moth didn't reply. He climbed the metal steps back to the street. The cigarette was still burning in his right hand. Fibres of smoke uncoiled across his view, faint nerves that, fading, made the inert background seem able to suffer.

The night bus left from Colmore Row when the flashing digital clock sign above Snow Hill read 0004. Initially filled with vivid shirts and drunken bickering, the bus was nearly empty by the time it reached Northfield. As it rocked, the distant streetlamps shook in the wind. The upper deck was cold, and smelt of alcohol. The bus, rarely stopping, wound its gradual way through a placid suburb. Semi-detached houses with front gardens and hedges; oak and cedar trees; churches with small graveyards. On the far side, a housing project with six new tower blocks, divided by car parks. Moth got out and crossed the main road to the nearest block. It contained fifty-six identical flats; his was on the ninth floor, near the top.

Inside it was like a hostel: plastic-covered stairs and whitewashed walls. However long you lived there, the effect of repetition never wore off. Moth only recognised the ninth floor because the girl in flat 42 had written TRORMA on the wall in jagged black letters, to inform the block that she was having a bad day. Many of the tenants were of Moth's age, transferred here by the Council from youth hostels or detention centres. Outside the door to his flat, Moth looked down the stairwell to the ground floor: a composite image of stairs and railings, like a fossil ammonite preserved in limestone.

Matt was waiting for him in the back bedroom of the flat. The static warmth and darkness of the room folded itself around Moth like a cloak. Without speaking to Matt, who didn't like words in any case, Moth lay down on the couch and folded his arms over his chest. The floor between the couch and Matt's bed was covered with litter, most of it things that Moth had brought in to occupy his mind. The alarm clock in the corner of the room flashed off and on, like the sign beyond Colmore Row. Brightness replaced distance.

When Moth's breathing indicated he was asleep, Matt levered himself upright and crawled steadily across the floor until he could fold his hands over Moth's face. He crouched there in the dark, his fingertips absorbing images from Moth's eyes as the boy dreamed. It was like reading Braille.

There was a code to the eye movements that Matt knew from practice. But lately the dreams were more complex than before. Matt sensed an element beyond the pattern of images he was used to. Moth was finding new hungers and needs of his own. Beyond the need for light, for the various powers of vision, the double needed power to control and damage. He needed to inflict pain. This was the best time, when the double started to become human. But it meant the threat of losing him altogether. Then Matt would be left to face his daylight as it really was: another darkness.

Darren was charmed but uneasy. The dance floor was too bright, and the music seemed to get louder with every track. He'd been working all day – Monday was his day off, not Saturday – and was finding it hard to relax. You'd expect YTS hairdressing to include cutting hair, but all he'd done for months was make tea, wash towels and sweep the floor. He'd finished the day with tears in his eyes. But tonight, he hoped, would make up for it. The boy he was dancing with was a complete stranger. A few others in the club had smiled at him, but he didn't seem to know any-one. He called himself Moth. Darren supposed that was because of his looks: a slim face with hair bleached nearly white, delicate bone structure and hollow, dark eyes. His eyes never kept still. As they danced, Darren had the feel-ing that Moth wasn't watching him or anyone else in par-ticular, but rather everyone at once, marking every pose or gesture for some private reason.

The lounge, next door, was quieter. They sat down with their drinks at one of the little white tables – like a cafeteria, Darren thought – next to the rockery set in one of the walls.

Water, faintly scented with disinfectant, trickled down the uneven rock surfaces to a ditch just below floor level. Patches of the grotto were lit in sky-blue, mauve or green. Moth didn't say a lot. 'Do you work?' Darren asked him.

'No,' Moth said. 'I sleep. And watch TV. And go out.'

'What do you watch?'

'Films.' He drew into himself. The continuous movement of light on the water held his attention more than Darren could. Minutes passed; Darren felt himself shut out.

'Why did you dance with me?' he said, half to himself.

'Because I like you. You're nice.' Moth lifted one hand and touched the side of Darren's face, for a moment as though he couldn't see it. 'You're really sensitive.'

'How do you know?'

'I can tell.' Moth let his hand drop back to the table. 'Look at the colours in the water. It's beautiful, isn't it?'

'I think it's a bit tacky. I'd rather look at you.' Darren could feel the vodka-and-tonic going to his head. He let the two parts of his mind separate. The side that knew he was being used couldn't be reconciled with the side that believed in it; so they faced away from each other. He let Moth's silence invade him.

'Do you smoke?' Moth tilted a pack of Marlboro cigarettes at Darren, who shook his head. Moth struck a match, lit the end of a cigarette and drew on it; he exhaled so gently that the smoke seemed to hang in front of his face like a veil. From the next room, Darren could hear the amplified voice of a drag queen singing 'As Tears Go By'. The cabaret had evidently started. He listened, and felt the energy and purpose draining from him like the smoke from the tip of a cigarette which left a stick of ash to crumble. With a soothing gesture, Moth flicked his hand over the ashtray; then he smiled at Darren. 'Do you live alone?'

'No. I share a flat with my older sister and her boyfriend.' He sighed. I don't get on with them. You?'

'I've got my own flat.' Moth paused, trapping Darren with his eyes, then shutting them, using the smoke as a pretext. The sound of applause broke sharply through the fading music from the next room. For a moment, something stirred in Moth's face that hadn't been there before, and wasn't intended. The two stared at each other, feeling the room around them expand to a cavern. 'Will you come back?' Darren nodded. Moth leant forward to stub out his cigarette in the ashtray; the movement brought their faces together.

The streets outside felt more oppressive than the club had been. Massive office buildings, without windows on the ground floor, soaked up the lamplight. The grey walls were crusted with dirt and the remains of half-scraped posters. On the corner of Livery Street, an old-fashioned urinal was a cell of rusty iron. Cars passed by slowly, their solitary drivers on the lookout for business. To get back into the centre of town, Moth and Darren had to cross the dual-carriageway where it came out of the tunnel; rather than trust the subway, they walked across, climbing the five-foot crash barrier in the middle. The cars and lorries emerging from the tunnel, on their way out of the cities, stared with the brilliant, multi-faceted eyes of insects.

The night bus cost them a pound each, but it was cheaper than a taxi. It left Colmore Row at two a.m. Moth relapsed into silence, staring at the road ahead. Once again, Darren had the feeling of being shut out, or worse, of being alone, in the presence of someone who was not present. He zipped up his leather jacket and pressed his arms into himself, trying to feel complete. The bus rattled and jolted its way through the empty roads in Northfield. Trainee bus drivers often used the night service to learn the route.

As the bus came back onto a main road, Moth got up silently and led Darren down the stairs to the door. They walked across the car park, an eerie sea of gravel in the lamplight, with a block of flats on either side. This housing estate was like a piece of inner city transplanted to the suburbs. In the building where Moth lived, a few windows were lit, too few to guess the number of storeys. The darkened rooms didn't exist from outside. In the lift, Moth put one hand on Darren's neck, while his other hand pressed the button for the ninth floor – three times, like someone dialling the police on one of the new public telephones.

Moth's flat had a clean, impersonal look that reminded Darren of a cheap hotel. The walls were pale blue, the floor an ash grey somewhat lighter than the fabric-coated sofa and chairs. There were vivid prints of Van Gogh's *Starry Night* and *Road at Alyschamps* on the walls, as well as a poster of Rutger Hauer in *Blade Runner*. All three pictures were slightly out of true, suggesting that Moth was astigmatic. He had a stereo, and a small TV set with an indoor aerial. 'Do you want some coffee?' Moth asked.

'Thanks.' Darren realised he was exhausted. It wouldn't do to fall asleep too soon. Moth gestured towards the couch. He switched on the TV and turned out the living-room light. The coffee was strong, with a bitterness that made Darren's mouth sting. They sat together and watched some old film in black and white. Darren stared at the profile of Moth's face. This seemed the natural light for it. It occurred to him, quite suddenly, that he didn't know what was going to happen now. He shivered and tried to suppress the thought. Of course he knew.

Moth changed the channel in a few minutes: another film, in colour. Darren slipped an arm around the other boy's shoulders. Moth sat for a few seconds, completely immobile. Then he stood up and changed the channel again, back to the old film. He switched the sound off and put a record on the stereo. Sinéad O'Connor's voice resounded, alarmingly loud in the small room. It grew from a plea to a terrible outcry, shaking with helpless rage. The loss between the words swallowed the voice, and guitar chords fell into the dark without echoing.

Darren felt lost; he lacked the power to move. Moth was standing behind him, massaging his shoulders and neck with gentle fingers. As his hand passed in the air above Darren's head, something like a skein of black threads seemed to move with it, tighten and then break. Darren reached up, but Moth was on his other side. He couldn't seem to co-ordinate his movements. 'Christ,' he said. 'I'm really tired. Can we...?' There was no reply. Moth sat down beside him, watching the film. Twenty minutes passed.

When the film ended, Moth stood up, gripping Darren by the shoulder. 'Come on, let's go to bed.' The bedroom was small and rather cold. It contained nothing but a single bed, a wardrobe and a chest of drawers. They left their clothes in a single heap on the floor. As soon as they were in bed, Moth lit a cigarette. His chest and arms were thin, almost hairless; the duvet covered him up below the ribcage. 'Do you mind if we talk?' he said.

'Not really. What about?'

'About you.' Moth smiled. He was really quite beautiful, Darren thought. He slipped a hand along Moth's side, down to the waist; but Moth pulled away. 'Wait.' He caressed Darren lightly, both soothing and exciting him. 'Tell me about yourself. Where were you born?'

'Coseley. That's near Wolverhampton.'

'In a hospital?'

'I suppose so. Don't remember. Why?'

'What's the first thing you remember seeing?'

'Seeing?' Darren lay staring at the reddish glow of Moth's cigarette; the room seemed to contract around it. Moth's hand stroked Darren's neck as though looking for the vocal cords. Darren shut his eyes. 'I remember... we lived on the second floor in a big house, facing a park. I remember being carried up the stairs. There was a paper lampshade in the hall. My cot was next to my older sister's bed... The children used to draw pictures on the pavement with coloured chalks. They'd draw round their shadows, and then colour in the faces. I must have been two or three years old then. I used to walk along the low wall in front of the house.' He didn't recall ever having described these memories before, even to himself. They could as easily have belonged to someone else.

'You can't remember back any further that that?' Moth gazed at him seriously, his eyes swollen with dark. 'I'm sure you could, if there weren't something wrong. Some dreadful thing you won't let yourself remember.'

'I really doubt it. What could have happened?' Moth didn't answer. He reached across Darren to stub out his cigarette. Darren kissed him; they pressed together for a few seconds. Then Moth turned away. In the complete darkness of the room, he might as well have been absent. Darren coughed. 'Moth, what do you want from me?'

'What do you mean?' His face was invisible, but very close to Darren's. This wasn't fair at all.

'Is there anything… well, anything you want me to do?'

Moth laughed quietly. 'Will you dance for me?'

'What?' Darren bit his lip. *Fuck off*, he thought. Two could play at this game. 'No, I won't.'

'Go to sleep, then.' Darren rolled over onto his back and lay still. Moth lit another cigarette and blew smoke-rings at the ceiling. His breathing was slightly asthmatic. Darren could see ghostly images in the smoke: the still faces of children. He wanted to say something, but his mouth wouldn't form the words. His anger and lust were tangled together in a kind of uneasy mist that chilled him inside. *Help me*, he thought, and didn't know if he'd spoken the words or not. Moth got up and walked through into the next room. He put a record on the stereo. It sounded like three or four songs being played at once; Darren wondered if it was different parts of himself hearing the same song. He touched the wall, running his hands across it as though it could give him comfort.

When Moth came back into the bedroom, the other boy was crouched with his cheek pressed to the wall. His lips twitched in time to the music. Moth pulled his head forward and stared into the rigid face. Darren's eyes blinked, but saw nothing. Moth drew the head down onto his lap and stroked Darren's gelled hair. His fingertips were as light as moonbeams. Gradually, they teased out a mesh of silver and black threads from the head. Moth snapped the threads with his teeth, making Darren's legs and arms twitch. He laughed to himself silently. The laughter was like fire shining on broken glass, somewhere deep inside him.

Dawn came early; they'd only been in bed a couple of hours. Darren's eyes were already open. He coughed painfully and tried to get out of bed; but his limbs wouldn't obey him. He remained below the duvet, one arm crooked beneath him, the fingers digging into the sheet. Moth kissed him and murmured, 'Dance now.' Darren climbed to his feet on the bed and danced there, his limbs jerking, his neck loose. From the next room, the stereo pounded out its message of atonal love.

Three hours later, Moth pulled back the curtain and opened the bedroom window. He rinsed his face with daylight, thinking about freedom. It was time to live for himself now. Behind him, Darren was lying on the floor, his head near his knees. He was breathing more steadily than before. Moth reached down and shook him. 'Daz. Wake up.' Darren opened his eyes and stood up awkwardly. 'Come on. Do you want some coffee?' He helped Darren get dressed, then pushed him towards the door. In the kitchen, Moth turned Darren around to face him, and kissed him slowly. It was the first serious kiss he had given anyone. They sat at the kitchen table, drank coffee and ate thin biscuits with the image of a coffee pot and cup engraved in them. Then Darren got up to go to the toilet. Moth followed him into the hallway. When Darren came back out of the bathroom, Moth embraced him silently. He let some of his own face tear away, like cobweb, between Darren's fingers. Then he pushed open the door to the other bedroom, and switched on the light. 'Meet my other half,' Moth said, closing the door behind them.

What Darren saw in the middle of the room, by the light of a forty-watt bulb, wasn't immediately familiar to him. Then he remembered where he'd seen it before. It was like the Natural History Museum's effigy of a male human body, proportioned according to the density of nerve endings in the skin. A huge head with bulging eyes, sealed chalk-white by cataracts; a loose tongue in a great flap of mouth. Two massive hands twitching in front of the shrunken body, crouched on frail legs; the genitals heavy and swollen. He was moving slowly from side to side, breathing. Darren imagined he was touching, tasting, smelling the air with his skin. Around them, the room was dusty and slightly damp. The floor and all the furniture were littered with photos, magazines, items of clothing, some dry flowers and the bodies of dead insects. Darren turned back to Moth, and saw the boy suddenly flicker and blur, as though lit by a faulty strip light.

'This is the last time,' Moth said. 'Surely this one will do.' Darren realised Moth wasn't speaking to him. He tried to turn round, slipped on a magazine and fell onto his hands and knees. He stayed like that, rigid with shock, as the blind thing approached him. Matt ran one giant hand across Darren's face, leaving trails in the flesh. He drew in his tongue in order to speak.

'You'll only die,' he told Moth. 'You can't exist on your own.' There was silence. Moth stared at him, then at Darren. The alarm clock in the corner read 0839.

'Goodbye then,' he said to Matt. He shut the door behind him, then walked out of the flat. In the lift, he pressed his hands and face against the metal wall. It was a brilliant morning, outside. He walked on, a little unsteadily, up the hill to the bus shelter. Sunlight flared in car windscreens going by on the main road. Further south, there were hills and woodland. To the north, traffic converged on the city. Moth shivered as the light struck his face. He crossed the road just in time to catch the bus out of town.

———————

If the city has a centre point, it may be the New Street ramp, where the vendors of hotdogs or cheap photographic prints wait alongside the demonstrators with placards and hand-printed leaflets. Everyone entering or leaving the city via New Street Station passes along the ramp. That afternoon, a dozen or so lads were leaning out over the railings, with sunlight in their faces and darkness in their eyes. Darren stood with them and listened to the city's atonal chorus. Starlings drifted above the shops like flakes of ash.

He sensed no direction or purpose in the crowd; nothing but a vacant hunger, a passive rage that would not allow anything to remain human, or even to remain the same for long. Across the road, a series of clothing and beauty shops faced the line of bus shelters, occupied by vagrants and prostitutes, in the shadow of New Street Station.

Darren crossed the road and looked at a shirt with black sleeves and a pattern of roses and violets on the chest. He didn't know what it reminded him of. Smiling at his pale face in the shop window, he ran a steel comb through his hair until it stood upright. It was a nice shirt. But Darren had no money; he was only window-shopping.

Joel Lane was the author of two novels, *From Blue to Black* and *The Blue Mask*; several short story collections, *The Earth Wire*, *The Lost District*, *The Terrible Changes*, *Do Not Pass Go*, *Where Furnaces Burn*, *The Anniversary of Never* and *Scar City*; a novella, *The Witnesses Are Gone*; and four volumes of poetry, *The Edge of the Screen*, *Trouble in the Heartland*, *The Autumn Myth* and *Instinct*. He edited three anthologies of short stories, *Birmingham Noir* (with Steve Bishop), *Beneath the Ground* and *Never Again* (with Allyson Bird). He won an Eric Gregory Award, two British Fantasy Awards and a World Fantasy Award. Born in Exeter in 1963, he lived most of his life in Birmingham, where he died in 2013.

These stories first appeared in the following publications: 'Common Land' in *Darklands* (Egerton Press, 1991) edited by Nicholas Royle, 'Albert Ross' in *Panurge* 11 (1989), 'The Night Won't Go' in *Critical Quarterly* Vol 32 No.4 (1990), 'Thicker Than Water' in *Panurge* 18 (1993), 'Wave Scars' in *Sugar Sleep* (Barrington Books, 1993) edited by Chris Kenworthy, 'The Death of the Witness' in *Ambit* 126 (1991), 'Other Than the Fair' in *Maelstrom* 6 (1992), 'And Some Are Missing' in *The Sun Rises Red* (Barrington Books, 1992) edited by Chris Kenworthy, 'The Foggy, Foggy Dew' in *The Foggy, Foggy Dew* (Mark Valentine, 1986), 'Waiting For a Train' in *Darklands* 2 (Egerton Press, 1992) edited by Nicholas Royle, 'The Circus Floor' in *Nutshell* 11 (1990), 'The Earth Wire' in *Winter Chills* 3 (1989), 'In the Brightness of My Day' in *Panurge* 15/16 (1992).

The following stories were original to this collection when it was first published in 1994: 'The Clearing', 'Branded', 'An Angry Voice', 'Playing Dead'.

ACKNOWLEDGEMENTS (1994)

Thanks are due to the following for help, support and encouragement: David Almond, Martin Bax, David Bell, Veronica Bradney, Peter Burton, Ramsey Campbell, Mike Chinn, Simon Clark, Lynn M Cochrane, Peter Coleborn, Andy Cox, Pam Creais, David Cowperthwaite, Pete Crowther, Dad and Jenny, Ellen Datlow, Jeff Dempsey, the Doppelgängers, Sue Dommett, Paul Drohan, Russell Flinn, Georgina Hammick, Helen Hancock, Dave Holmes, Stuart Hughes, Dorothy Hunt, Steve Jones, Graham Joyce, Chris Kenworthy, Tom Lane, Des Lewis, Simon MacCulloch, Tim Mathias, Chris Monk, Chris and Pauline Morgan, Clare Morrall, Mark Morrell, Mark Morris, Mum, John Murray, Greg Oxnard, Keith Parsons, Jeff Phelps, Dave Reeder, the late David Rees, Deryn Rees-Jones, Tom Roberts, Nick Royle, Simon and Adrian, Jason Smith, Mike Smith, Gina Standring, Arthur Straker, David Sutton, Elly Tams, Mark Valentine, Karl Edward Wagner, Laurence Westwood, Conrad Williams, Jane Wright, Malcolm Wright and Dennis Zaslona.

Influx Press is an independent publisher based in London, committed to publishing innovative and challenging literature from across the UK and beyond.

Lifetime supporters: Bob West and Barbara Richards

www.influxpress.com
@Influxpress